THE WATCHER IN THE WOODS

No doubt about it. Somebody was back there.

Billy Sawyer turned and looked behind. He'd just emerged from the little forest that grew along the west bank of Rocky Creek.

"That you back there, Framp?" Billy called. There was no one visible between him and the woods, but he was sure he'd heard someone cough a moment ago. That meant that whoever it was probably was still in the woods, watching him through the trees.

But there was no answer from the woods. Billy frowned, wondering if he were wrong. But one thing was sure: he'd heard *something*. A rustling movement in the trees, and that cough. A masculine cough, muffled.

He rode back toward the woods. "I'm coming in!" he called. "Don't try to hide…I've already heard you and know you're there."

Still no reply.

Just in case, Billy drew out his Colt….

Other *Leisure* books by Will Cade:

HENRY KIDD, OUTLAW
STALKER'S CREEK
GENESIS RIDER
LARIMONT
THE GALLOWSMAN
FLEE THE DEVIL

SAWYER'S QUEST

WILL CADE

LEISURE BOOKS   NEW YORK CITY

A LEISURE BOOK®

February 2005

Published by

Dorchester Publishing Co., Inc.
200 Madison Avenue
New York, NY 10016

ISBN 0-8439-5519-8

The name "Leisure Books" and the stylized "L" with design are trademarks of Dorchester Publishing Co., Inc.

Printed in the United States of America.

Visit us on the web at www.dorchesterpub.com.

SAWYER'S QUEST

Chapter One

"Look, Papa!" Laurel Sawyer exclaimed, holding her thin arms up and waving them about to steady herself. "Look at me walk!"

Billy Sawyer, who'd been absorbed with stocking a shelf at the rear of the general store in which he was a clerk, turned and looked in surprise at his crippled daughter. Laurel was balanced in the broad center aisle of the store, her small and slightly clubbed feet pressing into the polished floorboards, her thin frame trembling at the effort of holding herself upright. She smiled at her father, but even the smile seemed to require straining exertion.

"Laurel!" Billy exclaimed, heading for her in a rush. "You shouldn't be doing that, honey . . . it isn't good for you to put your entire weight on your feet, without your crutches to help. Dr. Garber has told you that . . . remember?"

1

"But how will I ever walk if I can't stand on my own feet?" she countered, replacing her smile with a challenging frown. "And I *did* walk, just now . . . I'll do it again so you can see me. Watch."

And before he could reach her or even speak to forbid her effort, the girl grimaced and gave her small body a heave that shifted her weight to her left foot and simultaneously brought her right foot off the floor about three inches. She twisted her frame and caused the elevated foot to swing forward a few inches, then shifted her weight again, from left foot to right. Her twisted right foot hit the floor. Laurel grimaced more intensely, then vaulted forward again, lifting her left foot this time, swinging it ahead.

With a muffled little cry she went down on her right knee, her right foot unable to bear her weight, meager as it was. She hit the floor hard, and fell onto her side. Billy reached his daughter and knelt, reaching down to lift her. She rebuffed the attempt and would not let him help her up.

"Papa, I didn't do it then, but I did do it before!" she said, pulling herself up to a seated posture. "I *did* walk. I took three steps. Three steps without falling. You didn't see because you weren't looking."

"I'm sorry, Laurel. I wish I had been looking. I was just distracted by my work."

"You believe what I'm saying? You really believe I walked?"

It was a hard question. He could believe she had succeeded in keeping herself upright on her misshapen feet for a few seconds, and had lunged forward a yard or so without tumbling down. He doubted it had been "walking" in any realistic sense of the word, though. But he didn't want to say that to her quite so forthrightly, and add more discouragement to a child whose life was one discouragement upon another.

So he played the diplomat. "I believe that whether you really walked today or not, one day you will walk . . . and not just for three steps. You'll walk like any girl walks, strong and healthy, for miles at a time if you want to."

"After the surgeons work on me, you mean."

"Yes. You know what the doctor has told us, honey. There's no reason your feet can't be fixed. It just takes a surgeon who knows what he's doing. Like Dr. Price in Chicago."

"But we can't afford Dr. Price, Papa. That's what you always tell me."

"Actually, what I tell you is that we can't afford him *yet*, Laurel. That's a big difference. Someday we *will* be able to afford him. And as soon as that happens, we'll go to Chicago, you and me, and visit him. We'll set it up for him to operate on you and make you walk."

Her wan face looked sad, her eyes moist. "But how long will that be, Papa?"

"I don't know, honey. I wish I did know."

"You don't make enough money working here to pay for Dr. Price. You say so all the time. You say that what you really need is to have your own store. You can make more money with your own store."

"Yes, Laurel. That's right. And someday I'll find a way to do that. It's my goal, my dream. But buying or building a store of our own is just like Dr. Price and the operation: It costs money, and money isn't something we have much of right now."

A tear rolled down her face. "It's always 'someday,'

3

Papa. Never now. And it ain't fair, Papa . . . nothing is fair! You can't walk unless you can stand on your feet, but the doctor tells me not to stand on them. We can't have the money to fix my feet unless we have a store of our own, but we don't have the money to get a store of our own. So how will I ever get to walk, Papa? How can we ever afford to get my feet fixed?"

It was hard for Billy to hold back tears as he looked into his distraught daughter's face. He had no answers for her; she was right. It wasn't fair that a man could work hard every day and not have enough money to give his own daughter the gift of mere normalcy. The child wasn't asking much from life, only the ability to walk across a room or down a road like anyone else. Yet that was the one thing he could not give to her.

Sometimes Billy Sawyer wanted to shake his fist at the sky until something or someone gave him the answer to what seemed an entirely reasonable question: Why? Other times he was seriously tempted to put aside his own moral convictions and do whatever it took to get the money to help her, even if it meant robbery. So far he'd been able to hold himself back from such a radical step.

"Papa," Laurel said, regaining some composure, "maybe if we don't have the money ourselves, we could borrow it from somebody who does. Somebody who would let us pay them back when we could, later on."

"Borrowing money can be as hard as earning it, sometimes, if you don't already have a lot of money or possessions to back it up," he replied.

She seemed confused by this, and her eyes suddenly washed with more tears. "We've got our house, Papa. We could use that to back it up."

"Honey, that house ain't really ours. We rent it. We pay to live in it, but it belongs to Mr. Campbell. Borrowing the money can't be the answer for us right now. We need to earn more money of our own first. Then, once we've built some up, we would have money to repay a loan in case we did decide to get one."

"Then *that* ain't fair, either!" she said. "If you got enough money to pay back with, then you wouldn't need to borrow it to begin with!"

Billy said, "There's not much in life that is fair, Laurel. People learn that as they grow up. Sorry to say, I think you're learning it earlier than most."

"But why did God set things up that way, Papa? Why didn't He want to make life be fair?"

"I don't know, Laurel. I truly don't."

"Maybe Preacher Jolly knows. He knows all about God and stuff."

"Maybe . . . but I suspect he doesn't really know that answer any more than we do. I suspect nobody knows the answers to some questions."

"When I get to heaven, I'm going to ask God why He made it so I wasn't able to walk without crutches. I'm going to ask Him what it would have hurt if I'd just been able to walk around like everybody else," Laurel said. Then she paused, thinking. "You know, Papa, in heaven I *will* be able to walk. Won't I?"

"Of course you will. But you won't have to wait until then. We'll find a way to get you that operation. We'll fix it so you can walk while you're still living in this world."

"You promise, Papa? Because if I could walk, then I think this world would feel just like heaven to me."

He knew better than to make her a promise, because

a man couldn't always predict what he would and would not be able to achieve in life. But this was Laurel, his beloved only child, the only living legacy of his late wife, Mandy, who had died when Laurel was very young. So he forced out a smile and said, against his better judgment, "I promise, Laurel. But for now, let's get you back on your crutches. We want to be careful not to hurt your feet. We want them to be as strong as they can be when you have that surgery."

His words brought a happier expression to Laurel's face. He was talking as if the surgery she wanted so badly was just around the next corner. He sensed her interpretation of his words, and it saddened him, because he hadn't meant to convey the impression that their situation was going to change quickly.

So he said, "Of course, Laurel, it will still be a while before we'll go to Chicago. I'll have to find a way to pay for it, and that will take time."

She saddened again, and nodded. "Maybe we'll meet somebody nice who has a lot of money, and they'll pay for it," she said. Then she frowned in thought, as if realizing something. "Papa, what about that man who's in town tomorrow? Does he have a lot of money? And is he nice?"

"What man are you talking about, Laurel?"

"You know . . . that man who is supposed to be in town tomorrow, over at the library. The one who writes books."

"Oh . . . Charles Oliver Farnsworth, you mean."

"Yeah! That's the one! Does he have money?"

"I'm sure he does, dear. He's written many successful books, books bought by people all over the world."

"Hundreds of them?"

"Thousands . . . thousands and thousands, in fact."

"And he makes money when those people buy his books?"

"I don't know exactly how it works, but I think that he makes money every time somebody buys a copy of one of his stories."

"Have you ever bought one of his stories?"

"Yes, a couple of them. And I've read other books of his that have been put into magazines, a chapter a month."

"Do the magazines pay him for his stories when they do that?"

"I'm sure they do."

"You think he's a nice man?"

"I've never met him. But he probably is a nice man."

"Then maybe he'll give us money for me to have an operation. Or for you to get your own store."

"Honey, it wouldn't be our place to expect him to do something like that, or his place to feel obligated to do it. Charles Farnsworth travels the world, and no doubt meets hundreds of poor people with situations they can't fix by themselves. People worse off by far than we are. He can't be expected to solve their problems. This surgery of yours is something we have to find a way to do ourselves."

"Maybe someday, though, *somebody* will help us. It's a good thing to help people, right, Papa? So somebody might do it someday, even if they don't have to."

"It is. And maybe someday we'll be able to help other people ourselves."

"That would be nice. I could find some other girl like

me, and help her have the money to go to Dr. Price, too. Wouldn't that be nice to be able to do?"

"It would, honey. It truly would."

Home for Billy and Laurel Sawyer was a small, rented clapboard house near the edge of town, about a half-mile's walk from the store where Billy earned his meager living.

It hadn't been so hard before Mandy died. Mandy had been the local schoolmarm, a job she almost lost when she married Billy because it was against local ordinance for teachers to be married. But the town fathers, recognizing her outstanding skill as an educator and the lack of anyone to replace her, had granted a variance from the usual policy so that she could continue to teach. Only when she had gotten pregnant with Laurel did they force her to resign. The loss of her income, small as it had been, made a major difference to the Sawyer family. Then, after her death, their situation had gotten even worse. It was Billy's fault, and he knew it. He had turned to liquor to find comfort for his grief, and had he not, in a burst of clear thinking, seen what he was doing to himself and for Laurel's sake turned off the drunkard path, the alcohol would certainly have destroyed him.

Billy could be strong when he had to be, and the knowledge that his daughter, deprived of her mother and even the ability to walk and live normally, deserved at least a loving and devoted father, was sufficient to motivate him to put the liquor aside completely. He would always remember that day of decision. He'd stared at a bottle of whiskey on the table before him, only about three swallows of liquor remaining in it, and he'd told himself that once that bottle was empty, he would throw it away and drink no more.

But as he'd stared at that tiny volume of whiskey, he'd changed his plan. Not even three more swallows. He had to stop *then*, not later. So he picked up the bottle, carried it outside, then slowly tilted it over.

He poured out one swallow's worth, then two, then in a final moment of weakness poured the final one into his mouth. He held it there, then in an exercise of fierce willpower spat it out onto the snowy ground. Not since that day had he touched another drop. Even when he was lonely beyond description and the little house was dark and Mandy's absence was so palpable that the air felt too heavy to breathe, he'd resisted the urge for whiskey. When the temptation was too much to bear, he would rise and go to where his daughter slept. He'd look down on her and, in seeing her sleeping face, find the strength to hold on.

He was proud of his sobriety, but wise enough not to let pride make him complacent. It would not be hard to slip, to buy another bottle, to fall back onto the same dangerous path he'd managed to leave. Liquor's grip could be strong. Billy had seen that for himself both in his own experience and in the life of Mandy's brother, Frampton Rupert, who lived just over the county line, close enough to this town that he could see the west side of it from his yard.

Billy and Laurel walked slowly down the boardwalk, Laurel's crutches clumping along steadily. With her crutches she walked with assurance and ease; she'd had a short lifetime of practice to perfect that skill. She could make it through life as a cripple, if she had to—Billy had satisfied himself of that—but he knew she hated being different than other people, hated being a slave to her crutches and doomed to a life of being pitied.

He would find a way to get her the surgery she needed, no matter what it cost him. He *would* find a way.

They reached the end of the boardwalk and stepped down. Laurel stumbled a little and Billy reflexively reached out to steady her. She pulled away. She never liked to be helped because it reminded her that she was different. "Sorry, Laurel," Billy said softly.

She pulled ahead of him; the girl could move quickly on her crutches. He watched her swing along, moving swiftly toward their house. He prayed for her, and for himself. *Help me to be able to help her, God.*

The street curved slightly, and as she rounded the curve ahead of him, he lost sight of her a few moments. During that time he glanced around, and noted a movement behind the window of the library. Mable Kirkell, the librarian, was working late. Getting ready for the next day's big event, probably.

Billy had to admire her. Just an old widow woman, wife of a local blacksmith who had been as rough and uncultured as his wife was well-read. She'd loved abrasive old Horace, though, and his death had devastated her. She'd held herself together despite it, and stepped forward from her private and reclusive life at home to become the local librarian, the first in this town of Rockfield, Kansas. She'd impressed Billy Sawyer . . . he believed that Mable Kirkell had done more for the education and cultural advancement of the town than had any other single individual he could think of, except perhaps for Waldo Morris, the wealthy rancher who had funded the library's construction.

Mable, though, had achieved beyond all reasonable expectation in snaring the great Charles Oliver Farnsworth for a visit to the Rockfield Library. She would hardly have brought a more famous man to town if she'd attracted the president himself. Farnsworth was an Englishman by birth, but his mother had been born in New York and Farnsworth had an abiding and deep love for his maternal homeland. The last three of his wildly successful novels, in fact, were set in the United States, and American readers accounted for most of his sales and personal fortune. But his forthcoming, in-progress novel, the newspapers said, was not set in America, a fact that reportedly worried Farnsworth and his publishers from a commercial standpoint. Would American readers take to a European story with the same fervor they had his American tales? To help ensure they did, Farnsworth was making an American tour, visiting major libraries across the country for public readings and discussions of his most famous works, and excerpts from his novel-in-progress, *Mortimer Straw*. *Major* libraries . . . so Billy was quite unsure how Mable had managed to persuade the great writer to come to such a backwater as Rockfield.

Whatever his reason for coming to Rockfield, Farnsworth's motivation behind the tour as a whole, Mable had explained to Billy, was to enamor Americans of him and his new book sufficiently to guarantee they would purchase many copies of it and maintain his international success.

Billy wished his own worries were so trivial. What would it be like to have only to worry whether your already great fortune would grow a little or a lot? What would it be like to have all one needed . . . to be able to take one's daughter to the surgeon she required, and simply pay for him to give her new legs and a new life? Billy could only dream of such a happy state of affairs, knowing even as he dreamed that all indications were he would never be able to make that dream a reality, despite his promises to Laurel.

Chapter Two

The only hotel in town stood across the street from the library. It was just ahead on Billy's right. It was small, only two stories, but the long second-level balcony porch lent an illusion of size to the structure. Hearing a soft scratching sound from above, Billy stepped off the boardwalk, into the street, and looked up at the balcony porch. Just as he did so, the wind gusted, blowing little whirlwinds down the street. Something fluttered into the air from the porch above, and floated, twisting, down toward Billy. He reached but was not able to catch it. He did see, though, that it was a piece of foolscap paper, with writing all over one side. It blew into the street and danced along in the wind, which was higher and stronger than Billy had bothered to notice until now.

"Damn and blast!" said a resonant voice from above with the accent of an Englishman. Billy instantly scrambled toward the paper blowing across the street, for he realized what it probably was, and *whose* it probably was.

He did not turn to look at the man on the balcony porch until he had chased down the paper. It was covered by very precise, neat writing, almost mechanistically perfect. At the top of the page was a page number and the words MORTIMER STRAW.

Good Lord, Billy thought. *In my hand I'm holding an actual page of an unfinished Charles Oliver Farnsworth manuscript!*

He looked up at the man on the porch, smiled at him, and waved the paper to show he had it.

"I caught it, Mr. Farnsworth!"

"Good man! Good man! You've recognized me, I detect."

It was indeed Farnsworth, looking as regal and British as Billy had anticipated he would. Farnsworth stood just behind the porch railing, a pencil in his hand and a stack of papers on the seat of the chair behind him. Atop the papers, to save them from the same fate as the page Billy had just rescued, was a metal case, lid standing open.

"Yes, sir, I do recognize you," Billy said. "And let me welcome you to Rockfield. We are honored that you've come to visit us."

"Ah, well, thank you," Farnsworth said, reaching down to accept the manuscript page Billy extended up to him. "Glad to be here . . . no part of this land so thoroughly American as these plains regions, in my view. And I do love America, even if it is not the land of my birth."

"You are free to consider it your homeland if you

wish, Mr. Farnsworth," Billy said. "Or at least your second homeland. That's the grand thing about America . . . we are built by the contributions of many people from many lands. If you wish to be an American, you may be one."

"Thank you, Mr. . . ."

"Sawyer. William Sawyer. Most call me Billy."

". . . Mr. Sawyer. Just like Twain's famous Tom, eh? Quite a thoroughly American name, to my mind, Sawyer is. And thank you, Mr. Sawyer, for your invitation to become a fellow citizen. Someday perhaps I shall make an official change of residence and citizenship. But for now I remain an Englishman content to be merely a visitor to this excellent clime."

Just then a burst of wind exploded down the street, kicking up dust into a stinging cloud. It hit both men, but Farnsworth had the worst of it, taking a load of grit in his eyes that caused him to grope reflexively, squinting and tearing up and taking a step backward on the porch deck. As he did so his heel bumped the metal case lying on top of his stacked papers, and the wind tugged a few more sheets loose and sent them blowing off the porch and down the street.

"Damned wind!" Farnsworth shouted, scrambling to save the rest of his manuscript from a similar fate.

Billy scrambled, too, going after the blowing sheets. He caught three, lost one . . . then remembered Laurel. Had she made it to the house before this wind kicked up? He'd seen Laurel knocked down in a strong wind more than once. She might be floundering on the ground even now, crying vainly for her father to help her.

Ignoring for the moment the busy Farnsworth, who was cramming his stack of papers inside the metal case,

Billy ran around toward his house. It came into view; he paused as the wind kicked more grit into his face, and looked about for Laurel. No sign of her. Then he saw a curtain inside the house move, and vaguely made out her silhouette behind it. Good. She'd gotten inside already.

He returned to the hotel porch, where Farnsworth was closing and latching the metal case. Billy thrust the papers upward. Farnsworth, eyes still gritty and wet, blinked and leaned down to accept the pages.

"Thank you, sir. The loss of even a few pages can be quite serious for a writer. It's virtually impossible to recreate them with any exactness once the originals are gone."

"I can imagine that would be the case, sir," Billy said as Farnsworth relieved him of the pages. Farnsworth stood, smoothing the wrinkled pages, then glanced down the street, squinting into the wind. "Blast this wind!" he declared. "Is it always so in this portion of the country?"

"There's often a wind here," Billy replied. "But that one was a stronger gust than most, and I'm concerned by it."

"How so?"

"The weather seems to be taking a turn. Quite unstable. And at this time of year, such conditions can lead to twisters. Cyclones."

"Dear God! Do you think one is on its way?"

"No, no . . . but the conditions could turn on us. I've seen it happen."

"You've seen twisters?"

"I have. Two years ago, I watched one lift five large cattle off a field, one of them with a bull mounted on its

16

back, and fling them to earth so violently they were all killed."

Farnsworth seemed dutifully impressed by the story. He wiped more dirt from his eyes and said, "I suppose the bull, at least, left this life as a happy creature."

Billy grinned. "Depends on how far along he'd gotten, I guess."

"Indeed, Mr. Sawyer. Indeed." Farnsworth laughed and looked down the street again. His laughter stopped abruptly, Farnsworth's face took on a startled expression, and Billy turned to see what had just captivated the famous man's attention.

Billy saw nothing unusual, just a lone man walking down the boardwalk on the far side of the street and turning into the Rockfield Tavern, one of the town's three saloons. The man was too far away for Billy to see well, but his posture and manner were familiar. It was Joe Spradlin, local blacksmith and farrier. Just a harmless local whom Farnsworth couldn't possibly know. Why had he reacted so to him?

"Dear God!" Farnsworth said beneath his breath, still staring down the street.

"I take it that you know Joe Spradlin?" Billy asked.

"Who?"

"Joe Spradlin . . . that man who just went into the saloon. The one you reacted to seeing just now."

"Spradlin . . . no. I don't know any such man."

"Yes. A local man, blacksmith."

"Oh." Farnsworth looked relieved. "I thought that was someone else. I'm glad I was wrong."

Billy was ready to move on and catch up with Laurel.

"I hope to see you at the library tomorrow, sir," he said. "Thank you for visiting our town."

Farnsworth nodded. "Glad to do so, sir. And then from here, it's on to Dodge City to lecture at a new music hall. Mine will be the first nonmusical performance . . . though words possess their own music, in my view. Well-crafted ones, at least."

"Indeed they do, sir," Billy replied.

Farnsworth tugged at his collar, looking up. "There's an odd feeling in the air, don't you think?" he said. "A sense of something precarious."

"Yes." Farnsworth was right. Billy had lived through enough Kansas storm season weather to detect that subtle instability in the atmosphere that indicated conditions were fertile for dangerously bad weather. Billy's desire to rejoin his daughter increased.

"Good evening, Mr. Farnsworth," he said, moving on toward his house. "I shall see you at the library tomorrow."

Billy sat up late that night, and Laurel did as well, because the wind was simply too strong and too frightening to let them relax. It howled around the eaves and buffeted the windows, working its way in around the edges of loose panes and causing the curtains to move, ghostlike. The fireplace, though dormant because of the season, exuded gusts of powdery old ash from time to time as the wind whipped down the chimney.

Laurel sat on the floor. Billy sat tensely in his favorite old chair, the only item of stuffed and padded furniture in the house other than the sofa, upon which he usually declined to sit. Usually Billy relaxed easily in this chair, often falling asleep in it long before he finally drifted off to his lonely bed, but tonight he was rigid, hands gripping the armrests.

"Papa, will there be a cyclone?" Laurel asked, watching another gust of ash burst out of the cold fireplace.

"It's hard to know, Laurel," Billy said. "This is the right time of year for it, but this town has stood here for years and never been hit by one, so there's no need to be unreasonably afraid."

"How about reasonably afraid?" she asked, and Billy was struck, as he often was, by a sense that his little girl had the mind of a much older person. Perhaps the trials of being crippled had a maturing effect on mental development.

"I guess 'reasonably afraid' is all right," he answered. " 'Reasonably afraid' is just the same as caution and awareness, I suppose, and those are good things. Don't worry too much, though. We'll keep our ears open. You can always hear a cyclone; they roar like a train rumbling on a rough track. If we hear anything like that, or see any other signs of problems, we'll just go outside and down into the shelter. That's all there is to it. We'll be safe in the shelter."

The shelter was simply an old dirt-walled basement that wasn't actually on the property Billy rented. It had been the cellar of a house that once stood next door. The house had burned and never been replaced; all that remained was the chimney, now a lone sentinel in an empty lot, and the slanted door that covered the cellar entrance. With the owner of the property uninterested in the place, Billy had simply adopted the cellar as a potential storm shelter for himself and Laurel. They stored a few items down there as well, though selectively, because Billy knew that, given his lack of actual permission to use the place, whatever he placed down there was subject to being taken should the owner of the property ever decide to make use of his lot.

The wind struck the house like Thor's hammer, and Billy said a prayer of thanks that the cellar was close. There was no cellar beneath the little rented dwelling he now occupied, no place he could feel his daughter would be safe if the worst came. That hole in the ground in the empty lot next door meant a lot.

"Why don't you go crawl in bed?" he asked Laurel, who had started badly when the wind struck.

"Can I just lie down on Mama's old sofa over there?" she asked.

Mama's old sofa. Billy smiled as she said it, but as he pictured the familiar but forever-gone sight of his beloved Mandy stretched out on that sofa, the smile became hard to sustain under a sudden onslaught of sadness. She'd loved that sofa, the best piece of furniture the two of them had ever been able to afford. But her essence, her persona, remained too attached to that sofa. He could hardly walk past it without imagining her there, and feeling the wrench of yet another realization that she was not. And that was why he could rarely bring himself to sit on that piece of furniture. It was a shrine, a concrete embodiment of a memory. But he didn't mind Laurel using that sofa. She was like a little bit of Mandy still remaining. She could use it without sullying it.

"Sure, darling," he said to Laurel. "Go ahead and lie on Mama's sofa."

She lay down, and he went to fetch a blanket from her bed. She gladly accepted the cover. The room was not cold, but the penetrating wind was uncomfortable and the blanket cut it nicely. Laurel closed her eyes and pulled the blanket up snugly under her chin.

Billy patted his daughter's shoulder and returned to his chair. Though the wind continued to buffet, Billy began to grow sleepy. He nodded, chin bobbing on his chest, ears still attuned to the weather outside despite his lethargy. When he opened his eyes again, it was very dark, and he was puzzled for a moment by the presence of a sleeping figure on the sofa across the room. Mandy? He almost called her name out loud, and then remembered, and sorrow came. It was Laurel on the sofa. Mandy would never sleep on that sofa again.

He closed his eyes, so lost in thoughts of his lost wife that he failed to notice there was now no sound of wind at all. The turbulence in the sky had settled, and there was nothing but peaceful quiet spread across the sleeping town of Rockfield, Kansas.

Billy shifted in his chair and fell into a deep sleep again. Sometime later in the night, he got up and made his way to bed, but Laurel remained where she was all night, greeting the morning still on the sofa that her mother had loved so dearly.

Chapter Three

Charles Oliver Farnsworth stood behind a podium borrowed from the local Methodist church, and spoke in the flowing accent of a well-bred Englishman, reading passages from assorted works that had made him a famous man. Billy Sawyer felt somewhat privileged, having met the man before, and having been acknowledged in the crowd by the great one himself as he came to the podium, so that now the others here knew the humble store clerk Billy Sawyer was acquainted, somehow, with one of the world's great literary figures.

Not that any but the local matrons seemed to care. Billy was the sole male seated in the crowd. The few men who had bothered to come out on this Saturday morning all stood around the edges of the room, looking disinterested and vaguely uncomfortable, some of them fidgeting as if they badly wanted tobacco. But Mable Kirkell's rule against smoking in the library was firm and never defied. "Makes the books smell bad," she always said.

Billy scrunched low in his seat, a little worried about being the only man showing much interest in Farnsworth. Was there something unmanly about literary interests? Odd, how much that bothered him.

As Farnsworth discussed the origins of his literary career and the "profound and telling influence" that Shakespeare's tragedies had had upon his mind and style, Billy's mind began to wander, attention floating across the room and out the east-facing window, through which the sun was struggling to beam. Though the sunrise had been bright in a clear sky, clouds had since moved in. Billy watched them, finding their color and apparent instability a little odd, a little distressing.

The calming of the weather that Billy had noted in the earliest hours of the morning was reversing itself. He thought of Laurel, probably still sleeping back at the house. He hoped she would keep aware of the weather and be prepared to head for the shelter if things turned bad.

He heard the wind rise outside, and the clouds scudded across the eastern horizon at a remarkable speed. Nervous, worrying about his daughter, Billy scooted around in his seat and tried to give the speaker at least enough attention to appear polite.

But it was hard. Farnsworth droned on, sounding increasingly self-absorbed, full of pride at his own achievements and fame. He seemed to assume that all were interested in his extended schedule, for he announced that he would travel to Dodge to give a reading of one of his novels in its entirety . . . a big endeavor, to be sure, but Billy could not imagine that anyone present at this moment would care enough to follow Farnsworth all the way to Dodge just to hear him read himself hoarse. Billy began to wonder why he had bothered to rise early on a Saturday just to witness a spectacle of self-aggrandizement such as this one.

Or perhaps he was merely jealous of Farnsworth's success. There had been a time in his life when Billy Sawyer had possessed some literary ambitions of his own. A book's worth of stories, a short novel, a stack of poetry . . . none of it had found its way into print.

Farnsworth opened a book and began to read. Billy squirmed. Nothing struck him as more silly than someone pompously reading his own words, as if that were something special in itself . . . as if the words had additional significance or meaning solely because they were spoken by the same person who had first thought them. Pomposity, it seemed to Billy. He'd left his daughter alone at home and come here to listen to an Englishman strut without walking . . . and meanwhile, the sky outside was becoming more frightening. Billy watched it more and more, and heard Farnsworth less and less.

Laurel Sawyer rolled over in her bed, eyes snapping open and breath catching in her throat. She sat up and blinked rapidly, wondering what had awakened her so suddenly. Wasn't it Sunday morning? Why hadn't her father awakened her as usual to get ready for church?

Where was her father, anyway? Typically she heard him moving around in the house when she woke up. But this morning the house was silent.

Though not entirely. There was a strange, continuous background noise she couldn't put a finger on. A hum, a whine . . . no, a howl. It was familiar . . . the same sound she'd heard last night. The wind, rising and moaning around the eaves of the little dwelling.

Her thoughts clarified a little. She realized she was wrong about the day. This was not Sunday, only Saturday. And then she knew where her father was.

That writer at the library. Farnsworth. Her father had planned to go hear his talk. And he'd left her to sleep late, as he sometimes allowed her to do on Saturdays.

She tried to settle back down and go to sleep, but the sound of the wind was too strong to let her do it. She huddled beneath her covers and stared at the wall, listening to the roar, and thinking that it grew louder by the minute.

She sat up again, eyeing her crutch beside the bed. Perhaps she should rise and dress, and be ready to leave the house for the shelter should the weather grow worse.

But what of her father? What if he was caught by the storm at the library? Perhaps he hadn't noticed the worsening weather. Maybe she should make her own way to the library, just in case.

But no. Papa might get angry if she left the house. He didn't get angry often, and usually his anger was quite restrained . . . but that only made her try all the harder to avoid it. When he got mad, it was usually for a good reason. She didn't want to give him a reason.

So she rolled over and tried not to listen to the wind. That proved impossible, but as time went by she did relax again, and her eyes drooped closed. Within a few minutes, she was asleep again. The wind howled louder, tugging at the edges of what consciousness slumber allowed her to retain, but it didn't quite make its way through.

In the library, meanwhile, Billy Sawyer rose and slipped toward the door. He bumped his chair as he left it, making a loud thump that drew everyone's attention and embarrassed him. He glanced apologetically at Farnsworth, who lifted one brow and gave him a quizzical expression in return.

"Mr. Sawyer? Have I driven you off?" Farnsworth asked.

The question, which had a toying quality about it, annoyed Billy. "No, sir," he replied. "My leaving has nothing to do with you or your words. I merely need to make sure of the welfare of my young daughter at home. The weather, you may have noted, is worsening.

"Is it? No, I had not noticed," Farnsworth replied. "I come from a land of cloudy skies, rain, fog, and gales. The weather is something I pay little heed to."

Billy looked around and saw that most of the others present were now looking not at him, but through the windows at the skies. From their expressions he realized he had been about the only person present who had his eye on the weather. This was surprising given that this was a crowd of Kansans who had little excuse for not recognizing cyclone weather when it presented itself.

They recognized it now. The men around the perimeter of the room grew agitated and looked both fearful and ashamed of themselves. They'd let a threat against their town, homes, and families develop and hadn't even taken note of it. Two or three men lunged into the crowd of seated women and grabbed at wives and daughters, telling them they must leave right away.

"Here now!" Farnsworth protested. "Must we disrupt all this in such a way simply because of some wind and clouds?"

26

"Sit down, Englishman!" bellowed Claude Monroe, one of the town's least cultured and most forthright citizens. "I'll not let a storm find me and mine sitting here in a blasted library, of all places, when it comes! I'm taking my kin to shelter, and you'd best find some for yourself, redcoat!"

"'Redcoat'?" Farnsworth repeated. "Mercy, sir, are we still fighting that old war here in the colonies? I made my peace with the American victory long ago, sir . . . in fact, I've become a great admirer of this free nation. Some consider me almost an American myself, and the American people—possibly with the exception of yourself—have embraced me and my writings most warmly. I hardly deserve to be spoken of as a 'redcoat.'"

"Well, no offense intended, scribbler. Now, if you'll excuse me, my wife and I will leave now. We need to get home to see to the safety of our family and our livestock."

The wind howled loudly and the building rattled. Farnsworth, startled, turned and stared at a shaking window. Everyone in the place was standing by this point, and several headed for the door.

Billy Sawyer led the way. He prayed that Laurel had already awakened and taken refuge in the old cellar. But he wasn't sure she would do that if she didn't know her father was safe.

He reached the door, muttered something to a man he knew, then left the crowd behind and raced, against a powerful wind, toward his home.

If it had been a living thing, it could have looked below to study the town it was poised to strike. It would have seen the line of tiny humans spilling out of the library and scattering in different directions on the street, the milling, weather-frightened horses in the livery pen, the wildly spinning windmill near the huge barn east of town. And the small, flimsy-looking house near the edge of town, toward which a lone man ran.

But the twister saw none of this, for it was merely a blind, steadily strengthening mass of circling air. It circled faster, faster, sucking into itself the vapor of clouds and taking on a slowly defining shape. The cyclone formed itself more quickly, almost as if with a conscious purpose, and began to descend.

The antlike humans on the street below scattered more quickly, heading for nearby buildings and cellars. The windmill creaked loudly, then broke away and spun off like a child's pinwheel. The sound of human screams of terror mixed with the scream of the storm itself. The street emptied of human life.

The cyclone mounted, then descended like the finger of divinity toward the town of Rockfield, Kansas, picking up grit and stone from the ground and making it part of itself. Its swirling, violent tip brushed against a shed beside the saddle shop at the end of Kirk Street and turned it into a mass of splinters and flying lumber, all of which the swirling monster incorporated into its being. Twisting ever more violently, driven by its own force, it moved on, in full contact now with the ground, and edged deeper into the little town, destroying as it went.

It happened too quickly for Billy Sawyer to fully grasp what was going on. He was conscious of running toward his house but seeming to go nowhere, struggling against a wall of grit-laden, violent air that stung his skin and made it impossible to keep his eyes open. Then he lost contact with the ground, feet moving beneath him but touching nothing. He let out a scream he could not hear because of the violent roaring of the wind, then tumbled once, twice, and struck hard against a resilient, cylindrical surface that knocked the wind out of him. He surmised, as best he was able to surmise anything in such a muddled situation, that he'd just been thrown against a telegraph pole or a wide porch column. He slid down the pole, whatever it was, and landed on the ground. In moments heavy material fell atop him, pinning him. He tried to struggle, the roar in his ears now slightly muted, but he could not move. Then the heavy material was yanked off him again and spun away into the sky. Billy tried to stand.

But he'd hit the pole hard, and was dizzy. He staggered and the great wall of wind knocked him down again.

"Laurel . . ." he said, though she was not near to hear. "Laurel . . ."

Then it was as if he were asleep. He saw nothing, heard only subconsciously, and lay still while the storm destroyed the town around him.

The funnel struck the library, which exploded like a huge bomb, sending huge shards of wood flying in all directions. Books flew as well, pages tearing out in the high wind and filling the sky like wildly flapping birds. Some rained down on the still form of Billy Sawyer, only to blow off again.

The cyclone lifted and drew up toward the clouds, but its energy was far from expended, so it began to re-form itself quickly. The renewed funnel dropped again, striking the hotel. Like the library before it, the building exploded, turning into flying rubble that violently circled and flew, some of it falling almost immediately back to the ground, the rest spinning off into the sky and out of sight.

Billy Sawyer saw none of it. For him there was only darkness, complete and dreamless.

From the perspective of the higher ground just across the nearby county line, one Frampton Rupert, brother of Billy Sawyer's late wife, had a good view of the destruction striking the town of Rockfield. For him it was entertainment of the highest order, and he was determined not to miss a moment of it. He'd dragged a chair from his house and sat it on the highest part of the low hill, then a bench from the shed that he used as a chairside table on which to place his bottle of whiskey. A tornado wiping out a town demanded viewing through a veil of alcohol, even if this was an hour too early for most to be in their cups.

Framp Rupert was not like most, though. He knew it and was proud of it. He'd never been able to abide rules, much less follow them. In Framp Rupert's mind, that made him not lower than other men, but higher. He was surely destined for greatness, success, wealth . . . and he would find it not by following the courses advocated in nursery, classroom, and church, but by going just the way they told him *not* to go. He was sure of it.

Ignoring the wind, he settled in his chair, uncorked his whiskey bottle, and poured himself a drink. He watched the distant, snakelike twister as it dipped down from a strange-looking cloud bank and touched a little shed, splintering it as if a bomb had exploded in its midst. Rupert started, sloshing his drink down his chin. "Damn!" he said in a sharp whisper.

A strong gust of wind struck him, along with a touch of rain, and he noticed something odd: Above his head, between him and the lowest gray clouds, objects flew. He looked up. What flew above were random things: sticks, shingles, bits of cloth, fragments of lumber. Things the tornado had caught and pulled high into the air, then flung off in the direction of the neighboring county and Framp Rupert. Rupert gaped as half a heavy chair flew above him and beyond the little hill to the plains behind him. Following it were several oddly flapping birds . . . one of which landed close to him and lay still on the ground. Rupert rose, and walked through the resisting tide of the rising wind to pick up the fallen bird.

But it was not a bird. It was a book. The flapping of its stiff covers as it hurtled through the sky from Rockfield had caused the illusion of birdlike flight. Rupert was no lover of literature, but could not resist picking up this volume. He squinted at its spine and cover, grit blowing into his eyes from the rising wind, and identified it as a history of France. A label on the base of the spine identified the book as property of the library over in Rockfield. Rupert looked inside the back cover to where those who had checked out the volume were listed. His eye fell on the name of Billy Sawyer.

Billy Sawyer. His own former brother-in-law. Or was he "former"? Was your sister's brother still your brother-in-law after your sister was dead? Rupert did not know.

Rupert stared at Billy's name, mouthing it to himself, then looked up toward Rockfield again. The twister was still alive, still in the town, but moving in Rupert's direction. He watched it demolish a barn, heave a wagon over a house, and pick up a goat for a high, fatal flight and fast descent. He was awed by the power of the wind.

Only then did he think the storm appeared to be striking hardest in the area of Rockfield where Billy and Laurel Sawyer lived. The library book he'd found was proof indeed that the tornado was in Billy's part of town. Though Rupert had never visited the Rockfield library, he knew it stood not very far from Billy's rented house.

Rupert stared at the tornado, trying to see exactly where it had struck, but because of distance, intervening buildings, and trees, he could not tell whether the little Sawyer house had been hit. He hoped not. A mixture of worry and guilt came over him, worry for the safety of his former in-laws, and guilt because he'd taken so long to think of them and realize the danger they might be in.

Not that Billy mattered all that much. He was no blood kin, after all. And Rupert didn't like him much because Billy, unlike Rupert himself, had managed to escape the prison of liquor. But Laurel . . . Rupert liked Laurel. Laurel had once resided in the womb of Rupert's own sister. She was his true kin, flesh and blood variety, and he should have thought of her and her welfare before now.

"You're nothing but a selfish ruffian, Rupert," Mandy had often told her brother. "You care about nothing but yourself and your liquor."

He'd always disputed her negative assessment of him, but deep inside he was secretly sure she was right. Indeed he wasn't a good man. Sure, he wanted to be one . . . but not all that badly. It was easier just to go on being what he was.

A cloud of fast-flying grit struck his face, stinging his eyes. He squeezed them closed and put his hands across his face protectively, but the stinging continued. Then a piece of wood hit him across the shoulder, the blow hard enough to nearly knock him over. He rose and ran, the wind pushing him, giving him unexpected speed. He tripped over a small stump and fell hard onto his chest, driving the wind from his lungs. He lay there a few moments, half stunned, then tried to push himself up. Just before his head rose, something big and heavy flew past, ten feet above, and crashed into the ground about twenty feet past him. It was a broken desk, or most of one. He marveled. Had it flown all the way from Rockfield?

The wind roared so loudly that Rupert couldn't sort out his own muddled thoughts. But he was able to realize he was in danger, that the violent weather he'd settled down to watch as entertainment had made a fast move in his direction. The twister itself might even reach him. And if not, the wind was throwing so much debris that he was at risk merely being away from shelter. His house, though, would offer little additional safety, especially if the cyclone actually came this far. He needed a cellar to hide in . . . or at least a ditch.

There was a ravine about thirty yards away to the southwest. He'd trapped many a rabbit there. Yes, the ravine. He'd be safer there.

Rupert stood, then fell again, pushed down by the wind. Now he got angry, and that strengthened him. Swearing, he pushed upright again, managed to keep his feet, and staggered toward the ravine. Something exploded behind him; he looked over his shoulder and saw the fragments of his woodshed, along with the pieces of firewood it had sheltered, flying skyward into a gray, swirling murk.

Rupert swore loudly—not that he could hear his own voice even at loud volume in such a roaring wind—then put his arms over his head to shelter himself from the rain of wood that came down upon him. He succeeded in saving his noggin from much damage, but a heavy chunk of firewood pounded his left shoulder so hard that pain throbbed electrically down his side, through his hip, and down his leg. He grunted and staggered; then his foot went numb and he went down to his knees. "Oh!" he said. "Oh."

He rubbed his shoulder, fighting the wind to keep from being blown forward onto his face. The wind prevailed and he rolled forward on his knees and found his face buried in the grass. Pushing up with blades of grass between his teeth, he cursed the storm that had been a source of dark entertainment, then got to his feet and staggered along with the wind shoving him between the shoulder blades.

"Dear Lord," he muttered. "It's hell come down from the sky. Hell from the sky."

The roar of the wind doubled in volume all at once. Rupert wheeled to see what was happening, and sucked in his breath in shock as he saw the cyclone driving right toward him. He froze like a terrified rabbit, and watched it come his way. The wind became so powerful he was forced back onto his rump and held there, unable to rise, staring at the twisting, dirty cloud. It seemed to be right upon him, though he knew it was farther away than it appeared.

After a few moments, the funnel cloud began to weaken and break apart. Rupert, not typically a praying man, breathed a word of thanks to the gray heavens. Then he found himself able to stand, the wind having declined. He rose, determined to get to a more secure place, and just as he reached his feet something descended from the sky and pounded his head like a sledgehammer, driving him down again, this time to pitch forward onto his face.

He lay there with eyes half open, staring across wind-whipped blades of prairie grass. His vision was out of focus, but with effort he was able to clarify it a little, and to see, lying almost with his reach, the thing that had struck him.

It was a box, not quite a foot in length and a little more narrow still in width. Clasps on its side held it closed. It was made of metal, and part of it had been damaged by the storm, bent back so that part of what was inside was exposed. A stack of papers. Just a metal, clasped box with papers inside. And it had found its way across the sky on the wings of the tornado, just to clunk Rupert on the head and leave him stunned nearly senseless.

His head ached, but he was also curious. When an item falls from the sky and nearly kills a man, the man wants to know what it was that hit him. So, with effort, Rupert pushed upward on the heels of his hands and tried to pull his knees forward so he could get up on them.

The effort strained him and made his head spin and swim. Woozy, he felt nauseated and weak, and with a groan collapsed onto his face again. This time his eyes closed and he went completely unconscious, the last thing in his fading vision being that metal box that had blown over from Rockfield. The wind was picking up again and the box was scooting along the ground, away from him. He saw it pulled into the air and carried off above the wooded hillside behind the house, perhaps to go find yet another head to fall upon on the other side.

Groaning, Framp Rupert closed his eyes. The storm passed over him, leaving him lying still, dampened, half buried in leaves and rubbish. It swept past his dwelling without harming it, then moved farther onto the plains, bringing rain in its wake and at last breaking apart for good.

An hour passed, and Framp Rupert slowly opened his eyes. Groaning again, he tried to remember where he was and what had happened. He blinked, for the clouds had dispersed and sun was shining through, warming his face. He struggled to rise and managed to roll over. There he lay another ten minutes, and finally got to his feet. He staggered toward his house.

Good Lord, what a storm! It was almost as if it had seen him sitting there on his little flat-topped hill, watching it destroying Rockfield, and had chosen to come chase him down and fling missiles his way for his insolence.

Remembering that metal case that had clouted him, he paused and looked around to see if he could find it. But it was long gone, carried off by the storm and probably desposited somewhere out on the plains beyond his house, where the twister had finally broken up for good.

Didn't really matter. He was curious about those papers, that was all. Papers stored in a closed metal case just might be valuable. Some kind of banking papers, maybe. Or property deeds.

Ah well. Whatever they were, they were gone. And

Framp Rupert had neither the ambition nor the strength to go looking for them just now. He entered his little house, threw himself down onto his bed, and fell asleep, his head aching terribly.

Chapter Four

It was three days after the storm. Billy Sawyer reached up slowly and massaged his closed eyes. It felt good, though the throbbing in his head continued like a discordant background melody. Playing counterpoint to it was the somewhat high-pitched, whining voice of the Rev. Charles Jango, pastor of the Rockfield Methodist Church.

". . . and at last his brother Willie found him," Jango was saying. Billy quit rubbing his eyes and opened them slowly, thinking he was being impolite by not looking at his visitor. But the light made his head hurt even worse. "Found James, I mean. Willie walked around behind what was left of the barn, and there he was—impaled. The twister had picked poor James up, thrown him all the way across the barn like a rag doll, and he'd fallen on the top of a splintered fence post. It pierced him through the lower part of his chest. There were ribs,

I'm told, pushed out his back, and his spine as well. And to think that Willie had to stumble across such a sight. You know how close he and James always have been."

"Yes."

"Must have been a terrible experience for Willie to find his own brother in such a horrible, mangled state."

"Must have been pretty bad for James, too. Dear Lord, what a death. Poked through by a sharp fence post!"

"Oh, yes. Yes. Not an easy way to die."

"I guess what you said when you first came in here was right, Reverend. Even though I got hurt a bit, even though my house got blown to splinter, I really was one of the lucky ones."

"Not lucky, Billy. That's not what I said. I said you were *blessed*. There's a great difference between luck and blessing. One is chance, the other Providence."

"You're right, Preacher. I misspoke. I am blessed. Blessed indeed. I lost my home, almost everything I possess, but I'm still alive. And best of all, my daughter is alive. And that is what matters most."

"It is. I thank God that he saw fit to spare her. Poor Mrs. Maddux lost her Emily, you know. Same age as your Laurel. She was crushed when her house collapsed around her. Poor child was home alone at the time."

"Laurel was home alone, too. But of course I didn't know a storm was coming when I left her there."

"Of course you didn't. And Mrs. Maddux could not have known, either. But she seems to be blaming herself."

"Had anything bad happened to Laurel, I would blame myself just as she is."

"We all would tend to think in that way in such a situation."

Billy looked around at the room he was in. On either side of his bed, blankets hung from the ceiling. Through the gaps between them he saw other beds, other blanket partitions. He and other people rendered homeless by the storm had been given temporary shelter in the church, which had come through unscathed. The place also doubled as a hospital. Though Billy was not badly hurt, the local sawbones had recommended he rest a couple of days because of concussion.

"Billy, what are your plans?" asked the preacher. "The store is gone, as you know, and I'm told there are no plans to rebuild. So you're without work."

"Yes. I don't know what I'll do in the long stretch, Reverend. For the immediate present, though, I have no choice but to turn to my late wife's brother, Frampton Rupert. He lives just across the county line. He'll take us in for a brief spell, at least. He's not overly fond of me, and he's got a rough side to him, but he cares about Laurel. She'd be safe at his house while I look for work and try to figure out what comes next."

The preacher nodded, but with a look of concern. "I've met Mr. Rupert. You remember when your lovely wife persuaded him to visit our church back at the start of her illness? I've never seen a human being look so uncomfortable inside a church house as he did that day."

"Framp has got a good share of sins to his record," Billy replied, smiling a little at the memory of the day the preacher had just mentioned. He'd never forget the way Framp had squirmed and fidgeted through what seemed an endless sermon, one that on that particular Sunday had focused on the grim wages of sin. Not a pleasant topic for a determined old sinner like Framp Rupert.

"Have you talked to Mr. Rupert about your plans?" the preacher asked.

"I have. He came to check on me yesterday . . . you weren't in at the time, Reverend, so you didn't see him. He had a close call with the storm himself. It passed over near his house, but spared it. And he was hit on the head by something or another. Knocked him half-cocked, but no serious damage, apparently. It was kind of him to come see me. Meant a lot to me, actually."

"Of course. Is Laurel already with him?"

"No. She's been staying with the Ellises since the storm. Kind of them to take her in, with a houseful of children already."

"They're good folks."

"Yes. And Laurel gets on well with their brood, so she's happy to be there. I don't know what she'll think of staying at Framp's place. She loves him as her uncle, but there's not a lot about his life and his home to offer much appeal to a girl her age."

"You will come through this, you know," the preacher offered. "Storms strike, *life* strikes, but with the Lord's help, we endure. And often come out better on the other side of it all."

"I know. I do expect we'll make it, Reverend. And again, thanks to you and the church for letting so many of us hole up here for a few days. It's good to have shelter."

"What better use for a church than to shelter its flock in a time of need? How long will you remain, Billy?"

"I'd be out of here already if not for the doc being so firm about me needing to rest. I don't see much need for it, myself. I got thrown up against a pole and took a good jolt to the skull, but I can't see why that should have me lying around in bed. I got no fever."

"He's a good doctor, Billy. Listen to him."

"I am. But I'll be out of here tomorrow. We'll gather up what little possessions we've got left, and head over to Framp's place."

"God bless you, Billy. And Laurel, too."

"Thank you, Reverend. God bless you, too."

The preacher turned to go, and Billy called him back. "Just wanted to ask you something. When the storm hit, the author Farnsworth was talking inside the library. I know the library was destroyed. What about Farnsworth? Did he get away?"

"Odd you should ask. I just learned the answer to that myself. Yes, it appears he did get away. He had left the library just before it went down. He was last seen racing out of town in that buggy of his, with the horse pulling it in a panic from the high winds. Jim Bland saw him drive over the rise north of town . . . and then the twister swept across right through that same area."

"Has anyone gone looking to see if Farnsworth was struck?"

"No one has found him, though a search was made. But they did locate a portion of his buggy. It had apparently been torn away by the wind. There was some assorted rubbish . . . a broken bit of luggage and so on. But no Farnsworth, and no horse. So apparently he made it out."

"Or was picked up and carried away."

"We shall hope not. I would not want our town to make its mark in history by being the death site of a famous writer. Too morbid."

"If Farnsworth is alive, I wonder what he thinks of America now?" Billy mused. "The sight of an American cyclone sweeping down at you and your buggy is bound to darken your rosy perceptions a bit."

"Indeed, Billy. And that would be a shame in Farnsworth's case. Though I'm not much of a reader of secular literature, one aspect of Farnsworth that I have appreciated is his profound respect for America. I hope he made it safely away from our town."

"So do I, Reverend."

It was a sight Billy Sawyer would recall vividly for the rest of his life. Framp Rupert's humble house, missing a little roofing here and there and looking rather battered, standing in the midst of a yard clearly damaged by the recent tornado, one tree fallen, ground torn up, trash and limbs everywhere. And in front of it all, standing with a smile across his face, Framp Rupert himself, wearing his worn-out old suit, his longish hair combed back neatly behind his ears. The old boy had dressed up for the Sawyers' arrival. It was his way of showing them they were welcome, and despite his usual minimal regard for Mandy's rowdy brother, Billy had to be touched by the gesture.

Billy was mounted on his horse, a fine chestnut that had come through the storm undamaged, safe in its stall. Laurel rode double behind Billy, one of her small arms around his waist and her crutches carefully held in the other. She peered around him and saw her uncle awaiting them, and Billy sensed when she smiled even though he could not see her face.

"Look at Uncle Framp," she said. "He's all dressed up!" Then she raised her voice. "You look nice, Uncle Framp!"

Billy nodded as he rode the horse right up into the yard. "You do look a fine sight, Framp. You didn't have to dress up for us, though."

"Well, a man like me don't often have reason to put on his finest. I figured this was as good an occasion as any."

His "finest." Billy thought it sad that a threadbare suit ten years out of style and dirty as a scullion's washrag was the finest that Framp had to wear. But the poor fellow had never had much money, and never would as long as he held to his drinking ways.

"Framp, thank you for welcoming us this way. And for letting us intrude on your home here."

"Well, Billy, what else would I do? Your home is gone. I can't let the loved ones of my own sister be without shelter, can I?"

"We appreciate the fact that you didn't."

"Hello, Uncle Framp," Laurel said, descending from the horse and steadying herself with her crutches

Framp smiled at his niece. "Laurel, howdy. Lordy, girl, you're looking more and more the image of your mother every day."

Laurel smiled shyly and headed off across the yard. She knelt and began poking at the shell of an old terrapin that was crawling across the ground. "That's old Jed," Framp said. "That old turtle is around this place all the time. I guess he likes it here."

Laurel picked up the terrapin, which immediately withdrew into its shell. She turned and smiled into the opening in which its head hid. "Hello, Jed!"

Billy came down from the saddle, walked up to Framp, and shook his hand. "Framp, it is a fine thing you're doing for us. I'll try to keep our time here short as I can, for I know you've got little space and are not situated well for houseguests."

"At least I've got a house to live in. I'm mighty sorry you lost yours, Billy."

"Well, I was able to save a few things. Including that picture of Mandy on our wedding day. You know the one. It was on the mantel." Billy paused and glanced over at Laurel, who was still engrossed with Jed the terrapin. "You're right about Laurel starting to look more like her. My girl's growing up on me, Framp. When I see her face sometimes I can see Mandy so clear in her features . . . it's almost like she was living again."

"It's a strange old world, Billy. Somebody sorry like me just goes on and on, and an angel like Mandy dies. It don't make sense."

"No, it doesn't. And it doesn't make sense that my little daughter should have to be crippled. Nor that a tornado should come down and wipe us out while we were trying so hard to improve our situation. Blast it all, Framp, it not only destroyed our house, but the store, too. And it won't be rebuilt. I'm left without work."

Framp nodded. "I know all about being without work. I'm that way half the time. I am right now, in fact."

"No cowboy work at the moment?"

"Not that I can get. The cattlemen around here know me too well, I reckon. They know I have a bit of trouble keeping myself away from the whiskey and beer."

Billy patted his former brother-in-law on the shoulder. "Framp, you'll shake off the liquor one of these days. You'll decide to give it a try and you'll succeed. I did. You can, too. Then things will turn around for you."

"Thank you for saying that. But I don't know I'll be able to shake it off so easy. Honest truth is, I don't think I want to bad enough, you know? I like it, Billy. Bad thing, I know, but it's true. I *like* it."

"Liquor, you mean, or being broke and in trouble half the time? For one goes with the other."

"Billy, don't preach at me. You were quite a drinker yourself when Mandy died."

"Yes. But I did see the error of my ways." Billy looked thoughtfully at Laurel. "I'm mighty glad my girl was too young to remember much about me in those times. That's not how I want her to think of her father."

"Yeah. Yeah." Framp looked off toward the horizon, very solemn and thoughtful. "Yeah," he said again. Then: "If I had a daughter like Laurel, maybe I'd have enough grit about me to straighten myself out."

"Well, you do have a niece like Laurel. And for a time she'll be living right under your roof. Maybe that will be enough to inspire you."

Framp smiled sadly. "I don't know that you'd really want that, Billy. The things a man goes through when he dries out, the things he sees and feels, and the things he says and hollers . . . not the kind of things you'd want Laurel to watch, I don't think."

Billy nodded. Framp had a point there. He said a quiet prayer of thanks that he'd been able to escape the grip of alcohol before it had gotten its claws as deeply into him as it might have.

"Well," Framp said in a brighter tone, "let's go inside and see what kind of a cook I am. I've got some pork I can fry, and some greens and such. And I do make a good biscuit, if I say so myself."

"Mind showing Laurel how?" Billy asked. "Laurel's

never been able to master biscuits, and I'm no good at them either, so I can't show her how to do it right."

"I make my biscuits the way my and Mandy's ma used to. The same kind of biscuits Mandy always made for you."

Billy's empty stomach grumbled. "Get inside and start cooking, Framp. I haven't had a biscuit like that since Mandy passed away."

They called for Laurel, and all went inside. Laurel took the terrapin with her.

Chapter Five

"Papa, they're arguing," Laurel said. "The big man looks like he's mad at Uncle Framp."

The girl stood on a footstool, steadying herself against the frame of a rear window as she looked out into the yard. She was surreptitiously observing her uncle Frampton as he talked with a man who had ridden to the house about twenty minutes earlier. The man was broad, shaggy-bearded, and quite tall. He loomed over Rupert like a great tree, and his fists, clenched tight and waving about as he and Rupert exchanged heated words, looked as large as Rupert's head.

Billy looked past his daughter and out the window, studying the scene. "Step down, Laurel," he instructed. "I don't want you watching that. Your uncle has been known to fight from time to time, and if he's building up to a fight now, I don't want you to witness it. That man is big enough to hurt Uncle Framp."

Laurel's face darkened with worry. "But you won't let that happen, will you, Papa? You'll go help Uncle Framp?"

"If it turns out he needs help, of course I'll help him, honey. But I'm hoping there'll be no fighting. Maybe they'll just argue out whatever they're talking about and be done with it."

"Who is that man, Papa?"

"I don't know. I've seen him before, riding through Rockfield. He's not the kind of figure you forget, once you've seen him."

"He's the biggest man I've ever seen, I think."

"Me too, Laurel."

"Why is he talking to Uncle Framp?"

"I don't know. Seems more arguing than talking. He's stirred up about something. Why don't you go on back in the house, Laurel? Find something to play with, your terrapin, maybe, or something to read or do . . . I'll keep an eye on what's going on outside, and if I need to help out Framp, I will."

Laurel obeyed, heading back into the rear of the house to play with her terrapin, which she'd named Oliver rather than keeping the name of Jed. Billy continued to watch the two men outside. The longer he watched, the less sure he was that he was witnessing an argument. Framp laughed a couple of times, for one thing, and the other man did as well. It seemed to Billy that perhaps Framp's visitor was simply a demonstrative man, prone to big gestures while he spoke, and some of what Billy had taken to be threatening behavior might not be that at all.

Still, he wondered what was going on, and the uncertainties he felt made him begin to question the wisdom of having come to reside with Framp, even for a short time. Framp lived a rough-edged life, not the kind Billy wanted Laurel to be part of, and Framp ran with a rough breed of people. And while they were here, Billy would have to leave Laurel alone in this place sometimes so he would be free to go out looking for work and a new place for them to live. What if some of Framp's rough friends came around while Billy was gone? Laurel might be terrified, or actually endangered, even as young as she was. Billy Sawyer was not naive about the terrible ways of some men.

Outside, the big visitor drew back his fist and seemed about to take a swing at Framp. But he merely leaned foward and tapped Framp lightly on the shoulder . . . a friendly-looking gesture.

Billy decided to go out and join them. If the visitor was here because of some problem involving Framp, Billy's presence might avert a brawl. And if he was here on a friendly basis, Billy could quit his worrying and relax a little. He took his hat from its hanging peg on the wall, plopped it on his head, and stepped outside.

Framp saw him coming and flashed a little grin. A smile of simple friendly welcome? Of relief that a potential ally and protector was joining him? Billy couldn't tell.

"Howdy, Billy," Framp said. "Junior, you know my sister's husband, Billy Sawyer? Billy, meet Junior Gaylord, good friend of mine."

Billy put out his hand. Junior put out his massive hand and shook Billy's, which was dwarfed by comparison. "Howdy, Billy Sawyer," Junior said, beaming and not looking at all threatening now that he was close-up.

"Junior," Billy said, hoping his hand wouldn't be

crushed by Junior's enthusiastic pumping. "Pleased to meet you."

"Good to know any kin of Framp's," Junior said. He seemed so warm now that Billy wondered how he could have perceived anything threatening about the man, even from a distance.

"Thank you . . . but I'm not direct kin of Framp's," Billy said. "My wife was his sister. Did you know her?"

"No, never got the chance. She's passed away now, I think?"

"Yes," Billy said sadly. Junior finally let go of his hand. "We lost her a few years ago, when my daughter was very young."

"I remember Framp here talking about it. Mighty sorry. How's your daughter doing?"

A noise back at the house made Billy turn. It was the door closing—Laurel had just emerged into the yard.

"There she is," Billy said. "She's crippled, but she's grown up well and has good health otherwise. She was too young to know her mother well enough to miss her like she might have if she'd been older. And she's smart as a whip, that girl."

"Takes after her uncle in that regard," Framp said, winking at the other two.

"Papa!" Laurel called.

"What is it, honey?"

"I just wanted to make sure you were all right."

"I'm fine, honey. Just talking to Uncle Framp and Junior here."

Laurel eyed the big newcomer. "Hello, Junior," she said. "I'm Laurel."

"Hello, Laurel," Junior said, smiling broadly and seeming sincerely flattered that he'd been greeted.

"Laurel!" Billy exclaimed. "Don't be rude. This is Mr. Gaylord, not Junior."

"I'm sorry, Mr. Gaylord," she said.

Junior was nonplussed. "Honey, don't you fret . . . I ain't been called Mr. Gaylord since . . . well, not since the last time somebody called me that. Junior's what I go by, and it don't matter how old the person is I'm talking to."

"I'm just trying to keep her respectful of her elders," Billy said. He might have added that he didn't appreciate Junior's undercutting his correction of Laurel, but thought that itself would be more rude than Laurel's familiarity in addressing a stranger by first name.

"I don't take no disrespect out of being called by my name," Junior said. "It's what my mama named me . . . why shouldn't folks call me that?"

"So you're not a junior because you have the same name as your father? Junior is your actual name?"

"Yes, sir. But it was my father's name, too. He was the first Junior Gaylord."

"That's right," Framp said. "I knew Junior's pap. Junior here is Junior Gaylord, Junior. Or Double Junior, as we sometimes call him."

Billy managed not to chuckle.

"I'm sorry I called you Junior, Mr. Gaylord," Laurel said.

"Nothing to be sorry about, Laurel. I mean, Miss Sawyer."

She smiled and wiggled her fingers at him. "Goodbye, Double Junior," she said in a voice intended to be too quiet for her father to notice. It wasn't, but Billy let it go.

"Billy," said Framp, "Junior here is a sociable man,

and a friend of mine for years, and he came over today to invite me to go with him this evening to a place we've grown fond of over the years. I'm talking about the Iron Forge Saloon. You know where it is?"

"I know it. Three or four miles south of here, right?"

"That's right. And Junior and me are going there this evening to have a few beers."

"You come too, Billy," Junior said.

"Yeah," said Framp.

Billy hadn't expected this. "Well . . . Junior, there's something about me you probably don't know. After my wife died, I took to drinking, way too much. And it was hard for me to break free of it. So now that I have, I don't go to saloons and places much."

" 'Much.' But you do go some?" Junior replied.

"I've had three, four beers in the last year."

"Good Lord . . . I could drink four beers in half an hour. You need to come with us, Billy. You need more beer in your system. Your health and well-being are at risk."

Billy smiled, but shook his head. "It's something I have to take pretty seriously, Junior. I can't let myself get trapped in the bottle again."

"So come have one beer with us. Maybe two. That's all. And we can talk about work."

"Work? What work?"

Framp cleared his throat and said, "Billy, Junior and me have both been thinking about the fact we need to make more money than we do. Junior's got some notions of how we might do it. Nothing you need to involve yourself in."

"I don't know about that, Framp," Billy said. "Junior, I'm without work myself, without a home, without a roof over my head except for Framp's. If there's work to be had and money to be made, I'd like to know about it."

"This may not be the kind of work you'd want to be in," Framp said, suddenly unable to look Billy in the eye.

"Oh," Billy said. "I think I see."

"Come talk with us, anyway," Junior said. "And we'll not let you drink more beer than you should."

Billy's mind worked fast. He didn't need to start frequenting saloons again, drinking away his worries and griefs like he had after Mandy died. And he surely didn't need to involve himself in anything illegal, but the undertone of what Framp and Junior were saying implied that some kind of crime was in planning.

Ironically, that made Billy more inclined to accept the invitation. If Framp was involved in something criminal, Billy wanted to know it. Perhaps he needed to get Laurel away from this place, before Framp did something that would bring law officers, armed posses and the like to the door. But he couldn't expect to learn about any planned criminal endeavor merely by asking. Framp would never admit to such a thing. Yet if he perceived Billy to be willing to go along with the scheme, then the truth might come out.

"I believe I might be inclined to visit that saloon with you men after all," Billy said. "One or two beers won't hurt me."

"Right, Billy," Framp said. "Maybe even three or four."

"But Framp . . . don't tell Laurel about it. All right?"

"Your secret is safe with me, brother-in-law. And with Junior, too. Right, Junior?"

"Right. Not a word to nobody."

"Thank you," Billy said.

The Iron Forge stood at the edge of a tiny community known as Forge Town. Both the town and the saloon derived their name from an old iron forge that had operated on the site in the early days of settlement. The saloon was located in a building that had once housed part of the forge operation, and since those early days had been much improved. The improvements hadn't endured very well, battered away over time by the rough and violent crowd that patronized the place. There were weekly fights at the Iron Forge, fights of all kinds ... shots fired, fists thrown, noses broken, bodies stabbed. Walls had been broken down more than once, and windows had only a short life span at the Iron Forge.

In his drinking days, Billy had visited the Iron Forge at least a dozen times, but his final visit had become just that because he'd witnessed a man being bludgeoned nearly to death inside the place. He'd seen other fights there before that, all of them fueled by alcohol. That was one of the things that prompted him to start seriously considering putting the bottle away.

And now, here he was, standing outside a place he'd vowed not to visit again, ready to go in and probably imbibe a little beer with two men he suspected were planning a crime.

"I shouldn't be here," he said aloud. "I think that twister may have done more than blow away my house and bust me up against a pole. It might have blown away all my common sense, too."

"Come on in. You just need a beer," said Framp. He put feet to his advice and led the way to the door.

The inside smelled like always ... foul and rotten.

Some of it was the spittle filling the saloons and staining the floor and even the tabletops. Some of it was the spilled beer that had permeated the floorboards. Some of it was the building itself . . . old and prone to leaks, stinking of dampness. And though he could not actually see any, Billy knew there was blood soaked into that floor as well, decaying and adding its own stink to the atmosphere.

And much of the stench came from the patrons themselves. Men of high culture, aqua fortis and rosewater these were not. They were to a man rough and rugged types, most of them in the cattle trade, some of them sodbusters or sheepherders. Billy Sawyer, the peaceable store clerk, felt a little intimidated by the folks who made the Iron Forge their own from night to night.

Framp found a table, and Junior, who fit right in with the Iron Forge crowd, headed for the bar and came back with a bottle of cheap whiskey, shot glasses for himself and Framp, and a tall mug of beer for Billy.

They sat down. Junior, beaming, poured generous shots for himself and Framp. Billy stared at his beer, trying to work up the courage to take the first sip, wondering all the while why he was doing this.

"Good Lord," Framp muttered, rubbing his head and frowning. "God, I don't think I'll ever be shut of this sore head."

"What's wrong with your head, Framp?" asked Junior. "No, wait . . . don't tell me. I remember. You got clouted on the noggin by some golden box falling out of the sky. Right?"

"That's right. But it wasn't no golden box. Just plain old metal of some kind or another. Brass, maybe."

"I haven't heard the full story about this," Billy said. "This happened during the tornado, right?"

"That's right. I was outside, watching the storm blow all hell out of Rockfield, and all at once, here comes this metal box falling out of the sky. Wham! Right on the head. Knocked me silly as a drunk Chinaman, I can tell you."

"Metal box," Billy repeated, looking thoughtful.

"Did you see what was in the box?" Junior asked. "If a box flew out of the sky and knocked me onto my ass-end, I'd want to know what was in it."

"It blew away again before I could get myself sensible enough to get up and get hold of it," Framp said. "But I saw it lying there on the ground for a little spell, some of the metal bent back. It had papers in it."

"Papers," Billy repeated.

"That's right. I wondered if maybe they were bank papers or something."

"Could be," Billy said. "But I might know what they are. I saw a metal box with papers in it myself, just the night before the storm, right there in Rockfield."

"What was it?"

"It was a box with a book inside."

"These papers weren't no book. They were loose, in a stack. Or so it appeared to me," Framp said.

"I didn't mean it was a printed book I saw," Billy said. "What I saw was also loose papers, what they call a manuscript. A book wrote out on paper before it's put between two covers and published."

"Then why do you know it was a book?" asked Junior, throwing back a big swallow of hot whiskey.

"The man who wrote the book had the box with him when I saw it."

Junior raised a finger as if to halt the conversation. "Hold on a minute," he said. "A man who wrote a book, in Rockfield the night before the twister. I know who that was, Billy. It must have been that famous writer fellow, that Farnswoggle."

"Farnsworth," Billy corrected. "And you're right. That's who it was."

Junior had just poured another shot. He drank down half of it in a celebratory way, congratulating himself upon being right.

"I knowed it!" he said. "I'm good at figuring such stuff out. And I've heard of that Farnswoggle. He's a mighty famous man. Mighty rich, too. I even read a story he wrote one time. In a magazine."

Framp snorted in mild contempt, then took a swallow of his own. "Junior, I never knowed you were even able to read, much less that you'd bother to do it."

"My own mama taught me to read before I was even old enough to commence school, Frampton," Junior said. "She said, 'Junior, we're going to sit down here together, me and you, and read this Bible story book.' And we did. And we did it again and again and again, days on end, until finally I could read that book all by myself. Why, I still remember it to this day. 'Lo and behold,' said the Lord. 'Adam looks right lonely. I'll make him a helpmate and name her Eva.' See? I did read it."

"You memorized it, Junior. There's a difference. And her name was Eve, not Eva."

"Pshaw! What does it matter? Point is I can read. You show me anything with words on it, right here and now, and I'll read it to you."

"All right. Read this." Framp pulled a piece of torn, yellowed newspaper from his inner vest pocket, and handed it to Junior. Junior squinted at it, picked it up, tromboned his arm back and forth a few times, then cleared his throat. Billy, meanwhile, could see the back of the paper scrap . . . a rendering of a pretty woman, smiling back at him from the yellowed paper. That picture was surely the reason Framp had torn out the scrap to begin with.

" 'Dr. Abel's Stomach Bitters and Digest . . . Digestive Aid,' " Junior read off an advertisement on his side of the paper scrap. "Pledged by its manufacturer to 'cure all dyspepsia, indigesti-onion'—or something like that—'and flatulence and afflictions of the annus.' " He stopped and looked triumphantly at Framp. "There, you see? I read it. Told you I could!"

"Hell, you read half of it wrong. What's this 'annus' you're talking about?"

"I don't know who she is. But I've knowed two women in my life who had that name. One of them was my own third cousin. Fine woman, my cousin Annus."

"I think the word in this case is 'anus,' " Billy suggested. "There's a woman's name, Annis, and then there's 'anus.' Very different things."

"The hell! You think I don't know my own cousin's name?"

"Oh, I don't doubt you on that. I'm talking about the word on the newspaper advertisement. That's 'anus,' not 'annus.' It says 'flatulence and afflictions of the anus.' See? Just one *n*."

"What the hell's an anus?" Junior said, far too loudly. The words all but reverberated in the saloon. He drew quick, odd looks from all around the room.

"Take a look in the mirror over the bar and you'll see one looking back at you, Junior!" called out a man

59

across the room, evoking laughter. Junior detected that he'd been insulted, even if he didn't yet get the joke, and nearly came out of his chair. "Dexter, you talk so to me again and I'll come make you wish you hadn't!"

"No offense intended to you, Junior," Dexter said, seeing the better part of discretion. "I just couldn't figure out what the devil you're doing in a public house like this talking so loud about your bunghole, that's all."

"My . . ." Junior trailed off, the pieces beginning to come together. "You mean *that's* what that word means?"

"That's right," Framp said. "Your anus is your bunghole." He grinned. "The pit of the valley where none dare to tread. The mouth that speaks never a falsehood."

"How'd we get onto this subject?" Billy asked, drinking a little of his beer. It was far better than it should have been and he took the next sip eagerly. *Already starting to slide in the wrong direction*, he thought. *I can't handle alcohol.* But he refused to let the thought take root.

"Oh, we got onto this subject by Junior showing off because he can read. You're a big old blowhard, Junior."

Junior, apparently trying to rise above the fray, looked at the newspaper again and said, "What's this here flatu-whatever thing this medicine claims to cure?"

"I'll demonstrate," Framp said, tilting himself to one side in his chair and doing just what he promised, loudly. "Hear that, Junior? Cousin Annus just said hello." He chortled loudly and Billy had to fight off laughter.

"Good Lord, man!" Junior said, glaring at Framp. "Smells like a privy in here now! I ain't going to sit here and breathe poison wind!"

Junior grabbed his whiskey bottle and glass and headed for another table, a small one off in a corner, where he could sit alone and not be plagued by such human crudities as Framp Rupert.

Framp shrugged. "I wasn't trying to run Junior off."

"Well, some folks just don't take well to having wind blown at them, I guess," Billy said. "I don't blame him much." He took another sip of beer, hoping his sense of taste would overwhelm his sense of smell, for the essence of Framp's offense still meandered heavily through the air. Unfortunately, the smell overwhelmed his taste buds instead, giving that sip of beer a revolting tang.

"Well, Junior'll be back. Me and Junior get on well with each other," Framp said.

"It's a good thing to have friends," said Billy. "Right now I wish I had more of them. Some who could give me work. I've got to find a way to get some money."

"Until you do, you and Laurel got a place with me."

"I much appreciate that, Framp. I'll try not to impose for long. I'll find work of some kind, somewhere."

"Sure you will. You've always been able to make an honest living one way or another, Billy."

"Not much of a living," Billy said. "But yes, I have been honest. Sometimes it's tempting not to be. Sometimes I can't help but think of what I could do for Laurel if I could get my hands on a pile of money all at one time. Even if it was stolen money. I could make Laurel able to walk, Framp! To walk! There's a doctor in Chicago who could operate on her and all at once her life would be different. Normal, like any other girl. No more crutches, no more falling down, no more feeling embarrassed when other little girls look at her the way they do, because she's not like them."

Framp looked at his former brother-in-law with a strange expression. Billy noticed, to his surprise, that Framp's lip had begun to quiver. When he spoke, his voice was tight, and Billy realized that Framp was struggling to hold back emotion.

"Is it really that hard for Laurel? Do other girls truly make her feel bad?"

"Some do. You know how folks can be, Framp. Harsh, centered on themselves, looking down on other folk."

A tear rolled down Framp's cheek. He quickly brushed it off and Billy pretended he'd not noticed it. But he gained a new appreciation for Framp, and saw him at that moment as more complete a man than he'd perceived him to be before. Mandy had always said that Framp had a side to him far better than the side Billy was accustomed to seeing.

"Billy, I want you to know that I think of Laurel almost as if she was my own. Hell, she's all that's left of my sister, and Mandy was all I had left of my whole family! My growing-up family, I mean. So she's mighty important to me."

"Thank you for saying that, Framp."

Framp stirred around as if uncomfortable. "Billy, you know what you said about having money to help Laurel, even if it was stolen money? How much did you really mean that?"

Ah, perhaps now things were getting around to the subject that Billy had suspected Framp and Junior were planning to talk about tonight. "Well . . . I don't plan to go out and commit a crime, if that's what you mean."

"I guess that would be wrong, wouldn't it? Committing a crime."

"I think that's pretty obvious."

"But if you were doing it for Laurel, how wrong would it really be?"

"I don't know, Framp . . . however wrong, it would still be wrong. I'm not a law-breaker."

"Well, hell! There ain't no fairness in the world, Billy. There's an innocent little gal like Laurel, just wanting to walk and be like any other one, and there's a way to help her, a doctor who can fix her right up, but you can't do it because there's no money for it. But the only good ways to get money, you can't do that either, 'cause it would involve breaking the law, stealing and such. It ain't fair. Life just ain't fair."

Billy grinned slightly. "You sound like Laurel. She gave me a similar bit of preaching herself not long ago."

At that moment, Billy's thoughts were interrupted by the sight of a man striding over to Junior's table. Junior looked up at the fellow and got a funny look on his face as the man, whose back was turned to Billy, said something to him.

Framp Rupert, noticing that Billy's attention was diverted, twisted his head around to see what Billy was looking at. He turned back around and said, "Well, looks like Joe Spradlin and Junior are back on speaking terms again. For the longest time they was all fell out with each other over that mule that Spradlin sold to some feller while Junior was scrambling to round up money to buy it himself. You remember that? Junior was set on getting that mule, and Spradlin knew it, but he sold it out from under him anyhow. Kind of mean of old Joe, I thought."

"Yeah," Billy said. "But that man there isn't Joe Spradlin. I thought he was, but when he turns his head a bit you can see his face, and it's not Joe. Just somebody that has his same kind of form and build."

Framp looked skeptical, but turned his head again and looked the fellow over more closely. Then the man himself turned slightly, his face showing now in profile. Just then Junior accidentally jolted his table, overturning the whiskey bottle and causing some to splash out on the man.

The man jumped back, cursing loudly. And at the sound of the curse, Billy was taken aback.

The man sounded just like the writer Farnsworth. Same tone, and exactly the same British accent.

Framp, having heard it too, looked back at Billy. "That man talks odd," he said. "You hear that?"

"Yes," Billy said. "It's a British accent. As strong a one as I've heard."

"British . . . hey, that ain't that Farnswoggle fellow, is it?"

"Farnsworth. It was Junior who called him Farnswoggle. And no, it ain't Farnsworth. But here's a funny thing . . . I was talking to Farnsworth the night before the tornado, him up on the porch of the hotel and me on the street. That was the same time I saw the metal box with his manuscript inside. Anyway, Farnsworth looked down toward the Rockfield Tavern, and you'd have thought he'd just seen Jesus Christ returning, or something like that. So I looked down, and all I saw was Spradlin, the real one, going into the saloon. But Farnsworth thought he was seeing somebody else, somebody *he* knew. And it was clear he wasn't glad to see him. He was very relieved to find out it was just a local man."

Framp rubbed his forehead and groaned. "Lord,

Billy, you're making me have to think, and with my headache thinking ain't coming easy. Makes my head hurt even worse to try."

"Sorry."

"But here's how it looks, then. Based on what you said, there's somebody out there Farnsworth don't want to see, somebody who looks a whole lot like Joe Spradlin, enough that when Farnsworth saw Spradlin, he thought he was really seeing this other fellow."

Billy picked up the strand of Framp's thought. "And now, we happen to see a fellow who looks like Joe Spradlin, but ain't, who has the same British accent as Farnsworth. So that fellow over there is probably the man Farnsworth thought he was seeing going into the Rockfield Tavern that night."

"Yeah . . . the one he wasn't glad to see."

"I'll be!" Billy said. "I wonder who this fellow is? And if he's following Farnsworth around for some reason or another?"

"Maybe so." Then conversation lagged as the Englishman turned and walked back out of the saloon. Junior watched him go, then happened to catch Billy's eye as he turned his attention back to his whiskey. Billy waved for him to come back over.

Junior did so, bringing his bottle with him. "I hope the air is fresher over here than when I left," he said.

"Clear as a springtime breeze, Junior," Framp said. "Sit down with us again. And tell us who that Englisher was talking to you just now."

Chapter Six

"Englisher?" Junior said as he lowered himself into the same chair he'd vacated earlier. "Is that why he talked so odd-like?"

"Yeah," said Framp. "What'd he want with you, Junior?"

"Well, truth is, he thought I was somebody else. Somebody who'd sold him a couple of horses two counties over. Charged him too much money, he says, and then one of the horses got sick and he had to have it shot. And when he told me that, I told him it was a sorry shame to shoot a horse before you give it a chance to get better, and then I spilled my whiskey on him and he thought it was done on purpose, and he got plumb mad at me. I thought he was going to draw a gun on me or something there for a minute. So he was an Englisher, was he? I never knowed any Englishers before."

"Did he say anything to you about Charles Oliver Farnsworth?"

"Old Farnswoggle? No, not a word. He just cussed me, mostly, for splashing whiskey on him. But at least I made him figure out it wasn't me who sold him the horses."

"Did he say what he was doing?" Billy asked. "Because I'm wondering if he's following Farnsworth around for some reason."

"Why you think that?"

Billy repeated the story of the porch and the sighting of Joe Spradlin, and Farnsworth's reaction to it. Junior poured and sipped some more whiskey while he listened. And Framp helped himself as well.

"Whatever is going on, I had a strong feeling that Farnsworth didn't want to run across this man. A very strong feeling."

Junior shook his head. "I tell you, if I were Farnswoggle, I wouldn't worry about nothing or nobody. I'd just spend my money, buy myself the company of the finest women, and be content."

"How much money has the man got?" Framp asked.

All eyes turned to Billy; he was the kind to know that kind of thing. But in fact he knew little. "I don't know . . . he's sold more books than just about anybody out there, so I guess he's a very rich man. But he roams and wanders . . . some of it promoting his books like he's doing now. Some of it, folks say, because he's on the run from something . . . a love affair, an enemy. But I've read a lot about the man and I don't tend to believe it. Because of the kind of stories he writes, folks are prone to want to make up things about him. And I think that's

67

all those kinds of tales about him are . . . just tales people made up."

Conversation waned a few moments. Billy wandered to the bar, and against his better judgment, purchased another beer. When he returned, Framp was gingerly rubbing his head and making a face of pain.

"Hurting where that metal box hit you?" Billy asked.

"Yep. I swear I think it cracked my skullbone a little."

"It probably did. You shouldn't work yourself too hard until that pain has all gone away."

"No worries about that," Framp said, grinning.

"Tell me, Framp, just where were you when that box hit you?"

"Out in the yard. That southeast corner of it. You know."

"Yeah. And then the box blew off?"

"The storm picked it right up and carried it over the hill."

"Over the hill. So it probably fell somewhere back there."

"I suppose so. Why?"

"Just wondering, that's all."

Framp squinted an eye at Billy. "You're thinking about going and finding it, ain't you?"

"Why would I do that?"

"I can think of a few reasons you might."

"Listen, I'm tired of talking. Let me finish my beer and let's just keep things quiet for a spell."

Framp looked slightly offended, but shrugged and took a big swallow of whiskey.

"And no more comments from Cousin Annus, all right, Framp? I don't want to have to walk away from you fellers again."

Framp grinned, hoisted his shot glass, and said, "No more comments from Cousin Annus. Or if there are, I'll warn you before she speaks."

No doubt about it. Somebody was back there.

Billy Sawyer turned and looked behind him. He'd just emerged from the little forest that grew along the west bank of Rocky Creek, the stream that skirted around Rockfield several miles to the east and flowed across the county line to the great meadow beyond the hill that stood behind Framp Rupert's house.

"That you back there, Framp?" Billy called. There was no one visible between him and the woods, but he was sure he'd heard someone cough a moment ago. That meant that whoever it was was probably still in the woods, watching him through the trees. And who else could it be but Framp? Only Framp knew he'd left the house, or would have any reason to come after him.

But there was no answer from the woods. Billy frowned, wondering if he was wrong. But one thing was sure: He'd heard *something*. A rustling movement in the trees, and that cough. A masculine cough, muffled.

Billy pondered whether to go on and ignore his hidden follower, or confront him. After a few moments' inner debate, he chose the latter option.

Unhesitantly, he rode back toward the woods. "Framp, I'm coming in!" he called. "Don't try to hide . . . I've already heard you and know you're there."

Still no reply. Good Lord, Billy thought, what if it wasn't Framp? Might Laurel have followed him?

No. That was not Laurel's cough he'd heard. Had to be Framp.

Just in case, Billy drew out his Colt as he rode into the

woods. The woods weren't particularly thick, and the storm had left many of the trees twisted and largely stripped of leaves. Still, there was enough foliage and shadows to provide some degree of cover to anyone who might wish to hide.

Billy moved quickly, hoping to unnerve the hidden one. But he found nothing, stirred no movement or noise. After five minutes he began to believe he'd imagined the entire thing, or that the hidden one had managed to exit the other side of the woods as Billy had entered.

Billy holstered his pistol, sighed, and turned his horse to go back to where he'd been. When he had turned, he sucked in his breath, startled. Another rider was there facing him, staring at him oddly, eyes flicking between Billy's face and his now-holstered Colt.

"Good God, Framp!" Billy exclaimed. "You just scared the life out of me!"

"Were you going to shoot me, Billy?" Framp Rupert asked. "You had your pistol drawed!"

"I didn't know for sure it was you, Framp. I couldn't take a chance."

"Why are you out here, Billy? What are you looking for?"

"Who says I'm looking for anything? I just took a ride, that's all."

"We know what you're looking for, Billy. You're trying to find that box of papers that clunked me on the head."

"Oh, is that right? Figured it out, have you? Why would I want that box?"

"Because of Laurel."

"Laurel?"

"Yeah. Because of her and all the things we talked about. You needing money, so that you can get her to that doctor in Chicago. And you figure that box has Farnsworth's book in it, and if you get your hands on it, he'll pay you for it."

"What do you mean, pay me?"

"Hell, that book is worth God only knows how much money! And unless he writes his books two times, it's probably the only copy he's got. So you figured you'd get your hands on them pages, and send word to Farnsworth that he can buy back his manuscript. Ain't that right, Billy?"

"No, Framp. It isn't right. I had no intent of holding that manuscript for ransom. That's no different from kidnapping, or extortion. But you're right. I did intend to find it, and try to get it back to Farnsworth."

"You were just going to *give* it to him? For nothing?"

"It belongs to him, Framp. It wouldn't be mine to keep."

"God! Ain't you the Sunday School superintendent all at once!"

"I won't lie to you, Framp. I have money motives in mind, too. I know that Farnsworth is a wealthy man. I know that book is valuable to him, like you said. So I figure it's likely he'd richly reward the return of his manuscript."

"He would if *I* took it back to him. I'd make sure of it!"

"You'd hold it hostage, in other words. Me, I won't do that. I'll count on the man to do the right thing by me."

Framp shook his head. "And I always thought you were smarter than me. Now I got my doubts."

"I'm not not smarter. Just unwilling to do something criminal in the name of helping my daughter."

71

"That wasn't how you were talking yesterday. You were talking about how tempting it was to get your hands on some money, no matter what it took to do it, so Laurel could walk again. Have you given that up, Billy? You going to let Laurel hobble around the rest of her days so you can feel all righteous about not getting money to help her from a man who has more than his share already?"

"'More than his share?' How do you figure that? What he's got he's earned, by the sweat of his brow."

"He ain't sweating all that much, scratching down words on paper. Hell, what kind of work is that?"

"It's *his* work. And that means the money he makes doing it is *his* money, not mine, not yours. Not even Laurel's. So just because he had the misfortune of having his book blown away by a tornado, I'm not going to demand something from him that isn't rightly mine. But if he wants to reward me, that's a different matter. That's his decision, his choice. One I'm counting on him making."

"You don't have the book, though."

"No, I don't," Billy admitted.

"What if you don't find it?"

"Then I don't find it."

"What if somebody else already has it?"

Billy frowned at Framp. "What are you trying to say, Framp? Do you have that manuscript?"

"I didn't say that. It's out there waiting for you, maybe."

"I'm not fond of the notion of looking for it with you trailing along behind me like a shadow. I'm not going to find that manuscript only to have you take it from me."

"Oh, I wouldn't do that, Billy. I mean, that wouldn't be right. I'd be doing you wrong if I took it."

"Sometimes people do wrong things."

"Yep. People do wrong things. So why are you so sure that Farnsworth is going to do the right thing and reward you for returning his book? Answer me that!"

"I don't know that he will," Billy admitted. "All I can do is hope. If I do the right thing and get him back his missing manuscript, maybe he'll do the right thing and give me a reward for it."

"Maybe he will. But me, I don't like *maybes*. I like to be sure. That's why my way is better."

"Framp, I'm going to ask you straight: Do you have that manuscript already? Did you come out here and find it sometime after the storm?"

"I've done chewed that cabbage, and won't again. Just keep looking, Billy. That's the only chance you've got to get your hands on it."

"Framp, I think maybe you *do* have that manuscript. And I think that you and Junior might have worked it out with each other to hold it for ransom."

"If that's true, and I ain't saying it is, then you know what I'd do with a part of that ransom, Billy?"

"Drink it away like you've drank away every other bit of money you've had, I guess."

"Some of it, maybe so. But some of it would go to get Laurel that surgery. So does my notion of holding that book for ransom sound so wrong to you now? If it will let Laurel walk?"

Billy was surprised by the strength of the emotion that crawled up his gullet, nearly choking him. "When my daughter has her surgery and walks again, it won't

73

be because somebody stole or extorted money out of someone. It will be because I pay for it with honest dollars. Not you, Framp. *Me.* She's my daughter, and I'll be the one who sees her put right, not you, not anybody else. *Me.*"

Framp drew in a long breath. "Very inspiring, Billy. I'm sure Laurel will be touched. Especially if you're not able to do what you want, and she ends up a cripple for the rest of her days."

Rage filled Billy. He reached for his pistol, a reflexive response to anger. Framp was faster, drawing his own pistol, a Remington, before Billy got his Colt clear of leather. He leveled it at Billy.

"Were you going to shoot me, Billy? Shoot the brother of your own late wife? Were you?"

"No, Framp. I wouldn't have shot you. I'd have restrained myself before I went so far as that. But I'll warn you: Watch your mouth when you talk about Laurel. And don't ever try to make it out that I'd do anything to keep her from getting better. There's nothing more important than that."

"Not even your high and mighty moral code?"

"I didn't say that."

"Yeah, you did. You said there's nothing more important than Laurel getting better. And nothing means *nothing*. No exceptions."

"Good Lord, Framp, I'm not going to bandy words with the likes of you. All I want is one honest answer from you: Do you have Farnsworth's manuscript?"

"No. I ain't got it. If I did, I'd be gone with it, seeing what kind of money I could get for it."

"Framp, let's put these pistols away. We don't want to be doing this."

Framp's brows wriggled like caterpillars. "No. No, we don't." He lowered his pistol, but did not holster it until Billy did.

Billy looked back into the clearing he'd been in before. "You think the manuscript blew out there somewhere?"

"Who can say? You know how them storms can blow things for miles. Hell, it might still be flying for all I know."

"But it looked like it blew it over in this direction."

"It did."

"Then I'll keep looking. But if I find that manuscript, Framp, there'll be no holding it for ransom. That's not the way I'll do business."

"Old Farnsworth may not be as kind and generous a man as you hope, Billy. He might take back his book, say thank you kindly, and that be all there is to it."

"I'll have to take that chance. I'm not a criminal. I don't hold people for ransom, nor will I hold people's possessions for ransom, either. It just isn't in me."

"Want me to help you look?"

"I'd just as soon you didn't. You know we'd just argue over it, maybe fight, if we found it."

"Yeah. I guess we would."

"Why don't you head on back to the house, then, Framp. Make sure Laurel is all right."

Framp nodded, and even managed to force out a grin. And Billy found himself thinking that, aggravating and no-account as his dead wife's brother was, he couldn't help but like him a little. And it all boiled down to the fact that Framp, like Billy himself, cared about Laurel. That was one of the few professions Framp made for himself that Billy had no trouble believing. Framp did love Laurel, because Laurel was family, and family loyalty was one of the few values Framp believed in.

Billy remained near the edge of the woods until he was sure Framp was gone. But even then he wasn't really sure.

Returning to the clearing, he resumed his search for Charles Farnsworth's missing manuscript box, knowing all the while that his odds of finding it were remote indeed.

Chapter Seven

"You were looking for what, Pa?" Laurel asked, looking up at her father with her big blue eyes shining in the flickering lamplight. Billy had just tucked her in for the night in the little bed that Framp had set up for her in what had been a messy back room used for storage and trash, but which Framp had worked hard to clean out so that Laurel could have her own quarters in his home. He'd even put a coat of cheap paint on the walls.

"I was looking for a box, a metal box, with loose pages in it. Mr. Farnsworth's book. I saw it the night before the storm, and the funny thing is . . . well, not funny, but strange . . . the same box, or what sure sounds like it, to hear Uncle Framp describe it . . . that same box was flung out of the sky and walloped Framp on the head while he was watching the tornado."

"Blowed over by the twister?"

"That's right. And after it hit Framp, it was picked up

by the wind again and blown away. Framp saw it flying off. It appeared to go over the hill and the woods, so that's where I looked for it today."

"Why are you talking so soft, Pa?"

"Oh, just want to keep this private, between me and you, that's all. Framp and I had a bit of an argument over how best to deal with that manuscript if we find it."

"What do you mean?"

"Nothing for you to worry about. Grown-up stuff."

"Pa, what would you do with that book if you found it?"

He chose his words carefully. "I'd get it back to Mr. Farnsworth, because it belongs to him and he needs it. It's how he makes his living, writing books. So with that manuscript gone away, he can't make money with it."

Laurel looked thoughtful. "Pa, is that box of papers valuable then?"

"Valuable to Mr. Farnsworth, certainly. And to all the people who love his books and would be disappointed if he never got that one into print because it was lost in the storm."

Laurel's eyes narrowed and a smile played at the corners of her mouth. She spoke in a different kind of whisper, and for a moment Billy was taken aback to see that his daughter had just taken on a resemblance in expression and sound to her uncle Frampton Rupert. She came by it fairly, of course, Framp being blood kin, but still it disturbed Billy to see it.

"Pa," she said, "Mr. Farnsworth might pay somebody for bringing that book to him."

Billy nodded. "He might." He paused, then found himself unable to resist going on and saying more than his common sense told him he should. "In fact, it is my hope that we might find that book and get it back to him, and perhaps get a reward."

"So you want to find that book to make money on it."

"Laurel, I hadn't planned to tell you this because it might build up hopes that don't come to pass. But my hope, honest truth, was that I'd find that box of pages and give it back to Mr. Farnsworth, and he'd be so grateful that he'd give us a good enough thank-you reward that we might be able to get on our feet again, and maybe even do some of the important things we've been talking about."

"Dr. Price?" she said, voice even softer now.

"Yes. But don't get your hopes up. There's no assurance we'll ever find that box; in fact, the odds are probably poor that we will. And if we did, we'd have to track down Farnsworth and give it to him. And he might not give a reward at all."

She squinted at her father and looked more like Framp than ever. "We could keep the book and tell him he could have it back if he gave us money. And we could even tell him how much money."

"Honey, that's not right, doing that kind of thing."

"It's not?" She didn't look angry, only disappointed.

"No, honey. It's a temptation to do, knowing that we could do good things with the money he might pay, but it just isn't right."

"Too bad."

"Yeah. But maybe we'll find that manuscript and he will reward us, not because we force it from him, but voluntarily. You never know, Laurel. It could happen."

She smiled, just a little. "Tonight I'll probably dream about walking," she said.

"Does it make you happy or sad when you dream that?"

"Happy, mostly. Because it makes it seem real. Like something that could really happen."

"One day it will, Laurel. It really will."

She smiled. He kissed her forehead, told her good night, and left her to sleep.

Whether Laurel dreamed of walking that night Billy never knew. But he dreamed of it. Dreamed of walking at her side up a church aisle, her tall and grown-up, wearing a white wedding gown while a preacher and groom stood waiting for her. No crutches. Just Laurel, whole and strong and grown-up, walking with not even a limp.

Billy woke up with tears in his eyes. He lay in bed a few minutes, dreading a future in which his beloved daughter would no longer be such a part of his life in the way she was now, yet looking forward to the time when she would enjoy normalcy, walking and running without impediment.

He rose and entered the kitchen, attracted by the scent of frying bacon. He walked in ready to pronounce blessings on Framp for preparing breakfast, but it wasn't Framp working and perspiring over the small iron stove, which had heated the room to an almost unbearable level. It was Laurel, who turned and greeted her tousle-haired father with a sleepy smile.

"Already made biscuits," she said. "The same way Framp makes them."

"Bless you, daughter!" Billy said.

"Amen," said Framp, grinning slightly at Billy. "Cooks as good as her mother did, just about."

Billy nodded, though it wasn't true. Laurel could handle kitchen duties well enough, but Mandy had been a cook beyond parallel.

"I wish you had a bigger stove, Uncle Framp," Laurel said. "It's hard to fit the skillet on this one."

"I know, Laurel," Framp said. "I had to buy the cheapest thing I could find. And I wish now I'd put it out in the shed and turned that into a kitchen. A stove's got no place inside a house. Heats it up too much."

"Not bad in the winter, though," Billy threw in.

"Guess not. But it ain't winter and it's got me sweating today."

The preparations were quickly done and they ate together at Framp's rough and too-small table. Too small for three, anyway. Framp's bachelor's dwelling wasn't well designed for company.

"I wish I could afford a better place," Framp said around the rim of his coffee cup. "This ain't bad when it's only me, but I can't be much of a good host with so little room."

"Laurel and I don't ask for much," Billy said. "This place is just fine. At least you've *got* a place, Framp. I miss our old house, even if it was only a rented dwelling."

"Yeah, yeah. Cussed storm! It ain't right that good folks can have things took away from them in such a way. You didn't deserve to lose your home."

"Well, it appears from observation that things like that aren't often decided based on who deserves what," Billy said, finishing off his eggs.

"If we could only find that book we were talking about, maybe we could get enough money for all of us to be set up," Framp said.

"If you're talking about that book by Mr. Farnsworth, Pa said last night that it would be wrong to hold that book for money even if we did have it," Laurel said.

"Yeah, he said the same to me," Framp replied. "And maybe he's right. But I tell you this: It also ain't right for folks like you to be in such a bad situation. Just ain't right."

"I don't think it's right, either," Laurel said.

"Well, it's all theory anyway," Billy said. "Right now we don't even have that book manuscript, so it's all just noise in the air."

"I wish I did have it," Framp said. "But I don't, dang it. I don't."

Billy spent part of the day looking for work and part of the day looking again for the box. By late afternoon he was tired of the quest and beginning to think it was silly, anyway. He'd never find that box. It could be anywhere across the wide Kansas landscape. And odds were it had blown open in flight and the contents had been flung far and wide, anyway. He headed back toward Framp's house, vowing to himself to forget the entire matter. He'd find some other way to rebuild his fortunes than the slender hope of charity from Charles Oliver Farnsworth.

He spent the evening reading an old newspaper he'd picked up in town, distracting himself from the failures of the day. He'd found no work, nor even the hope of any. It was beginning to dawn on him that he might have to pack up his few remaining possessions, put Laurel on a horse, and the pair of them head to other climes where maybe luck would be easier to come by.

Laurel had fried up a chicken for their supper, a chicken provided by Framp. Billy asked no questions about where Framp had obtained the chicken. He certainly didn't raise them. But stolen or not, the chicken was delicious, and Laurel received abundant and well-deserved compliments from both her father and uncle. Billy even volunteered to clean up the dishes afterward, just to thank her. He was glad she was finally learning to cook well, and for that, he knew, he had Framp to thank.

Laurel looked over the newspaper Billy had brought home while Billy finished washing up. "Pa," she said. "It talks about Mr. Farnsworth here, and the book he's writing."

"Does it? I missed that. What's it say?"

"It says that the book is called *Mortimer Straw*, and that he's coming to Rockfield to talk at the library." She folded down the paper. "I wonder if he knows the library is gone now."

Confused, Billy walked over and looked at the date of the newspaper. "This is an old paper, Laurel. That was written before the visit he already made. That's what it's talking about."

"Oh." She looked at the story again. "It says he was going on to Dodge City after Rockfield, and would stay there for two or three weeks."

"Dodge City?" Framp said. He'd seated himself in his favorite chair in the corner and was loading tobacco into a corncob pipe. "So if we find that book, I guess we'll be off to Dodge, eh, Billy boy?"

"I kind of think we won't find that book, Framp."

"We'd be rich men if we did."

"Rich? Doubt that. There might be some reward money, but nothing to make a man rich."

"Not your way. My way, there would be."

"You can't kidnap a book like you would some rich man's child. It's foolish, and it's wrong."

83

"Foolish? The man gets rich off his books. So they'd be worth a king's ransom to him. Just like his own child would be. Foolish? I don't think so. Wrong? I don't know. I'm not sure how much I care about wrong. Who's to say what's wrong, anyway?"

"How about God? 'Thou shalt not steal.'"

Framp stood and folded his hands in mock piety. "Let us now stand for the benediction. Reverend Sawyer, please lead us in prayer."

"This is absurd, Framp. Nonsense! Let's you and me make a bargain here: no more talk about that book. Because it's all wasted words. Fact is, we don't have it and probably won't ever have it. I wish the whole thing had never been thought of by either one of us."

Framp nodded. "You're right, Billy. You're right. We ain't got that book and we ain't going to find that needle in a haystack that's half a county big."

"And it's probably best we don't," Billy said. "I mean . . . folks, we're all the family any of us have got. We ought not fight among ourselves."

"You're right, brother-in-law."

"I'm always right, Framp," Billy said with a subtle wink.

"He thinks he is, anyway," Laurel said.

Ever since her mother's death, Billy had made a habit of tucking Laurel in at night, just to remind her that she was not alone despite the loss of her mother. It was a time he cherished with her, one he dreaded losing when she became too old for such little-girl sentimentalities.

He pulled the quilt up under her chin and brushed her hair back from her eyes. Bending, he kissed her forehead lightly. She smiled and he smiled back.

"I love you, Papa."

"I love you, Laurel." He bent and kissed her once again, then went to the door.

"Papa," Laurel said as he started to exit, "is it always wrong to tell a lie?"

He stopped, surprised by the question. "I suppose it is, honey, unless you're protecting someone's life or something like that. But wrong things can be forgiven, if maybe you've told a lie and that's what's on your mind right now."

She shook her head, face solemn. "It wasn't me. It was Uncle Framp. He said he didn't have that box of Mr. Farnsworth's."

"Are you saying that he does?"

"Yes. He's got that metal box. Or at least some metal box that's the right size to hold papers."

"You saw it?"

"Yes. I seen it. I seen Uncle Framp looking at a metal box like that, out in the shed, before you came home. I'd gone out this afternoon to scrape out some table scraps for that stray cat that's been coming around, and I saw him through the knothole. He had the box down and was looking inside it. Stacks of pages. I seen them."

" 'Saw' them, honey, not 'seen.' Did Framp know you saw him?"

"I don't think so. I was real quiet."

"I guess he doesn't know, then, or else he'd not have said at supper that he doesn't have it, for he would have known that you knew better."

"What do you think he lied for, Papa?"

"I don't know. But I suspect he might be planning to tell Mr. Farnsworth that he can have his book back if he pays a good bit of money for it."

"Think maybe Uncle Framp would let us use some of that money to get my legs fixed?"

"We couldn't take that money, dear. It would be wrong."

"Oh. Yeah."

"Thank you for telling me what you saw. You did the right thing."

"Papa, I don't want Uncle Framp to be mad at me for telling on him. Do you have to tell him I told you?"

"No, Laurel. I don't. But what I will do is 'find' that box myself. That way he'll have no notion you were involved at all."

"Is that just another kind of lying, Papa?"

"No, honey. We're not telling him a falsehood. We're just withholding information he doesn't need to know. I don't want him to be mad at you, either. He's family to you, the family of your own mother, and I want you two to get along well. It's important that family get along."

"What will you do with that box of pages after you get it?"

"I guess I'll try to get it back to Mr. Farnsworth. And hope he'll see fit to reward the deed. And if he does, maybe there'll be enough to take you to the doctor in Chicago."

"Oh, Papa, I hope! I hope!"

"But we don't know yet, honey. Remember, this is all just hoping for right now, not knowing."

"I know. But I do hope . . . real hard."

"Me too. Good night, Laurel."

"Good night."

The outhouse stood on the far edge of the backyard. Billy waited until the light in Framp's window went out, indicating he'd retired to sleep, and headed for the out-house.

On the way back he positioned himself where the shed hid him from view of the house. He circled the rear of the shed and slid inside. It was pitch-black, almost, so he took matches from his pocket and struck one. Its flare caught the glimmer of a lamp, so he took the lamp down, removed the chimney, cranked up the wick, and lit it. When the chimney was back on, the shed was filled with light.

Billy hoped that Framp wouldn't look out his window and see the light in the shed. If Framp found him out here, Billy would claim he'd come looking for some lamp wicks. The lamp beside his bed did in fact need one, so the story would be believable.

Framp did not come out, and Billy made his search of the shed without being confronted. But he had no luck finding the metal box Laurel had seen. Frustrated, he was about to give up, but spotted the knothole that must have been the one through which Laurel watched her uncle. Thinking logically, Billy evaluated the angles of view that she would have had through that knothole, and looked in those areas for the box, one last time.

And finally he saw it, up on a shelf, carefully hidden by assorted items set in front of it. Resisting the urge to brush the junk aside and get right to the box, he took time to memorize the placement of all the items that hid it. Then he moved them aside just enough to get to the box, which he lifted down and set on a little work-bench on the floor. Then he put the items he'd moved back into place so that it was almost impossible to tell without a close look that the metal box was no longer behind them.

By the light of his lamp he opened the metal box, which was quite bent up from its rough flight through the tornado. Inside he found, as he'd expected, the carefully scribed pages of *Mortimer Straw*.

Laurel was right. Framp had found the book. The blasted liar!

Billy was in a quandary. Should he confront Framp? Framp would probably try to claim ownership by merit of being the finder. Because he perceived the manuscript as fodder for ransom, Framp might even fight to maintain possession. One thing Billy didn't want was Laurel witnessing a brawl between the only real family members she had left.

No, all he could do was spirit the manuscript away and try to track down Farnsworth. But how? And when? If he took it tonight, Framp would find it missing the next day, and who could know what kind of reaction *that* might spark? On the other hand, if Billy took off with it tonight, he'd either have to take Laurel or abandon her, leaving her with only Framp to care for her. Either way, Framp would quickly discover that not only Billy but also the manuscript was gone, and probably come after him. Or he might actually hold Laurel as a hostage of sorts until Billy brought back the manuscript. Billy could easily imagine all kinds of intolerable scenarios, even Framp coming after him with intent to kill. Would it be beyond him, if he really believed that manuscript could make him a good bit of money?

Billy flipped through some of the manuscript pages, but was so distracted he could hardly make out the words. He closed the box, still debating his course.

He could reach no conclusion. He stood, stretching his back, watching his lamplight-cast shadow move on the wall and across the window. And then he saw another movement . . . *outside* the window this time. Or was it just his shadow playing tricks against the reflective cheap window glass?

Movement again . . . and this time Billy was sure. Someone was outside the shed, and had just looked in through the window, ducking away when Billy looked back.

Good Lord. Framp had caught him. Who else could it be out there?

No point in trying to deny the situation now. Framp would have been able to see not only him, but the manuscript box.

Billy steeled his nerves, cleared his throat, and pushed open the shed door. He stepped out into the night.

"Framp?"

No answer.

"Framp!" he said a little louder. This time there was a response, but not an audible one. Just movement on the other side of a tree about twenty feet from the shed. There was just enough ambient light to let Billy make out the heel of a boot and the curve of a man's calf clad in denim.

"Framp, I see you behind that tree. Come on out. No reason to hide."

The figure emerged, stepped forward. And Billy knew at once that it wasn't Framp. An entirely different height and build, but not unfamiliar.

And then the man was close enough for Billy to see. "Well!" he said. "Hello, Junior."

"Billy Sawyer, how are you this evening?"

"Quite well, Junior. You?"

"I'd be better off if I was a rich man."

"Wouldn't all of us!"

"So we would. But the sad fact is, only a few folks get rich. The rest get left out."

Billy frowned. Something odd in Junior's words, but he couldn't put a finger on it. The content? The tone? Both?

"Did you come to see Framp? Because I believe he's gone to bed. I saw the light in his window go out a little while ago."

"Yeah, I came to see Framp. But it's all right if I don't see him tonight. It appears to me you might be the man to see this evening."

"Why's that?"

Junior paused and scuffed the toe of one boot in the grass. He sighed loudly. "You know, when I came in and saw a light burning in the shed, I figured it was Framp in there. Looking at his little treasure. I was surprised when I looked in to see that it was you instead."

"Yeah . . . I came out looking for a lamp wick. The one in the room I'm sleeping in is no good. Smokes like a cheap cigar and gutters like a drunken harlot."

"Did you find a new one?"

"No. No, I didn't."

"But you did find something in there, didn't you?"

Billy stared.

"I know what you found, Billy. I seen it."

Saw it, Billy mentally corrected.

"You found Farnswoggle's book."

Damn! Billy thought. *He saw it, and knows what it is. I knew he and Framp had been scheming.* Knew *it!*

"I found a metal box with papers."

"Let's not play games with each other, Billy. You found that book . . . the book that Framp found earlier.

Same one that clunked him in the head. You know where he found it?"

"No. Tell me."

"In the woods out that way." Junior waved in the direction of the woods where Billy and Framp had gone through their little confrontation when Billy was out searching for the manuscript box. "It was lodged up in a tree. Blowed there by the storm."

"How long ago did he find it?"

"Don't know exactly. Sometime soon after you and your girl came to live here."

"We're not living here. Just staying for a brief time until I can get back on my feet again."

"And that's what you plan to use the book for, eh? Getting back on your feet?"

"I plan to take the book and give it back to its rightful owner."

"Farnswoggle."

"Farnsworth. That's right. And I figure there is a good chance that he'll be grateful enough to pay a reward for it."

"Maybe so."

"So Framp has had that manuscript for a little while now, has he? He's denied it firmly enough."

"He's been afraid you'd somehow take it away from him, and he considers it his chance to move ahead."

"I know. He wants to hold it for ransom from Farnsworth, and I'm against that."

"Yeah. But Framp thought you could be persuaded to change your mind. Framp and me have been talking for a period of time now about doing something to help ourselves out. Not necessarily nothing legal, either. Just something that has a good payday."

"Why hasn't Framp taken the manuscript and gone with it, if he's had it for some time?"

"Tell you the truth, I think it's because of your girl. She's got him around her finger, that girl does. He thinks all the world of her and told me that he hasn't run off because he doesn't want you making her think bad of him. The truth is, he's got it in his head that you'd figure out what he'd done if he ran off with that manuscript and tried to find old Farnswoggle, and that you'd tell the girl he was doing something bad. He doesn't want her thinking him an evil man."

Blast that Framp. Just when Billy had good reason to despise him for his bad ways, something from his better side asserted itself and Billy couldn't hate him.

But in the present situation, Framp was a problem for him. As was Laurel, and Junior Gaylord. All of them presented their own kinds of barriers to Billy doing what he needed to do.

If only he, and not Framp, had found the manuscript first! As it was, Framp would claim possession of it on a "finders keepers" basis. He might be willing to fight to keep his perceived key to wealth. And Laurel . . . she was an impediment simply because she had to be seen to, cared for, protected. Billy didn't want to abandon her here, yet would be slowed by her company if he took her along. A crippled child didn't make for fast and efficient traveling. And Junior . . . he presented a problem if only because he knew too much, and because he, more than anyone else, could intrude himself into this matter with little at stake. Billy and Framp both cared for the welfare of Laurel, which affected and limited their options. But Junior could take risks. If he took the manuscript and headed off on his own, it was likely he could successfully hold it for ransom and make away with the money, all for himself. Framp could do the same, of course, but his love of Laurel would cause him to share his gain for her benefit. He'd said as much, and Billy believed him.

"You planning to take that manuscript for yourself, Billy?" Junior asked. "Is that your notion?"

"I plan to use it, if possible, to see my daughter put right. I want to make money with it to have surgery done to make her able to walk properly."

"Well, that's a high calling, but it's Framp's possession. He found it first."

"It isn't Framp's possession. It's Charles Farnsworth's possession, and didn't stop being so because he lost it through no fault of his own."

"So you'll give it to him. And keep all reward for your own use."

"I'll keep it for the benefit of my daughter." Then inspiration struck. "Of course, I'd not keep it all. If the reward was big enough to pay for Laurel's surgery with some left over, I'd give some of it to Framp, as finder of the manuscript."

A moment of silence. Junior stared at him, his left brow rising and eyes becoming so piercing they almost seemed to glow in the darkness. He leaned a little closer to Billy.

"And some to you, too, Junior. If you'll come with me and help me find Farnsworth and get the manuscript back to him."

Junior stood taller all at once, looming down over Billy. "Hmmm! You'd have me go along with you, then."

"Yes . . . if you'll agree that there'll be no holding the

manuscript for ransom, only turning it in to its rightful owner in hope of reward."

Junior grunted again, thought it over a moment, and stuck out his hand. "Partners, then."

Billy, hesitant and very unsure of himself, shook the hand after a moment. "Partners it is, I guess."

Billy could not go without leaving some sort of explanation for Laurel, but she was asleep and he did not wish to wake her to tell her he would be gone for a time. So instead he wrote her a note that he carefully tucked beneath her pillow without disturbing her.

Laurel, dear,

I am going for a time. I have recovered the Farnsworth manuscript and am taking it to Dodge City in hope of returning it to Charles Farnsworth and obtaining reward for the effort. You know my hopes and dreams for what could be done with the reward, so please pray that I will find Mr. Farnsworth in a grateful and generous humor.

It is my hope that your uncle will not follow, for I can see nothing but strife coming of it. And so I must ask you to do something for me. If he does speak of an intention to follow me, feign illness. Tell him you are unwell and need his care, and I believe that for your sake he will desist from following. And do not worry that he will be harmed for not doing so. If there is sufficient enough reward I will share with him a good amount. And by keeping him from carrying out his ransom plan I may even be sparing him from the danger of prosecution and jail.

Pray for my safety, keep Framp at home, and I shall see you as soon as I can. Destroy this note without Framp's knowledge. And know that I remain your loving and devoted father always.

Billy gathered up some of his few goods, strapped on his pistol, and went to the barn, where Junior waited. Saddling his horse, Billy last of all packed the manuscript box into a saddlebag, belted it closed, and mounted. Then he and Junior rode away from the house in the deep night, heading for the road that led in the direction of Dodge.

Chapter Eight

Morning found Billy Sawyer exhausted. He'd been up and busy the entire day before, unprepared physically and mentally for a night of horseback travel. So when he and Junior made camp, Billy could hardly get his bedding laid before he was in it and fast asleep.

Junior was a different story. The man had an apparently unending store of energy, and made coffee rather than lie down to sleep. He sat drinking from a metal cup, occasionally glancing at Billy, his eyes moving often to the saddlebag that held the item they all hoped would put money in their pockets.

Billy was sleeping deeply. Junior could do it . . . he could get that manuscript and be gone, and Billy would not awaken. Then Junior could say the devil with Billy Sawyer, Framp Rupert, and the whole cussed world. He could track down Farnsworth alone, offer to sell him his lost manuscript, and take all the proceeds for himself.

But it wouldn't really be that easy. Billy Sawyer would be after him like a persistent shadow, threatening the success of a solo venture. And if Billy managed to get to Farnsworth first, he might say far more than needed saying, and Junior would face not the receipt of ransom, but the grim arm of the law. And even apart from Billy, there was Framp, who would have this thing figured out quickly and be on the road to Dodge himself, probably before this dawning day was done.

Junior had only two options: either kill Billy while he slept and be ready to kill Framp the next time he saw him; or go along with Billy as was the current plan, and perhaps manage to talk some sense into him. They could make much more money through ransom than they could hope for through reward. Junior fancied himself a persuasive man, and so hoped that by the time they reached Dodge, he could have Billy's mind changed about how to approach Farnswoggle. And why not take some of the rich old coot's money? What did one man need with all that money to start with?

Junior finished his coffee and was beginning to feel a little weary, but a wind kicked up and something came blowing down the dirt road. Junior looked at it, couldn't make out just what it was, rubbed his eyes, and looked again. It was a newspaper. Two or three sheets of it, partially entangled, blowing like a tumbleweed in the stiff breeze.

Junior got up and headed out to intercept the newspaper. Despite his earlier bragging to Framp and Billy in the saloon, he wasn't a very good reader, but with effort he could get by. And now he was in a reading mood. It was boring, sitting in a camp with just a sleeping near-stranger for company, and the only other handy reading material was Farnswoggle's book, which didn't interest him except as a source of cash.

He got all three sheets of the paper with one grab and hauled them back to where he had been sitting. Smoothing them, he spread them across his folded legs, then pulled out a cigar, lit up, and began to smoke and read.

The newspaper, to his surprise, was out of Dodge City. Carried miles away by some traveler and lost, maybe, or perhaps blown for many miles on the Kansas wind like that manuscript box had been. Whatever its origins, it was a recent edition, only three days old, in fact.

Junior read slowly, having to mouth out some words to make sense of them. He read about weather and church meetings, and crime news. Lots of crime news. Those were the best stories, the most colorfully written and lively. And then he turned a page and found himself staring at a story he'd not expected to find. He worked his way through the multi-decked headline and into the body of the story, and was more deeply entranced with every line.

When he was finished, he read the story again, faster this time because he'd been through it once already, and that second reading gave him a full comprehension of what he'd read. And hope that there would indeed be gold waiting at the end of the road he and Billy were now traveling.

Laurel woke up with the sun, not because of the light, but because a particularly noisy peddler drove by on the road outside, hollering loudly for Framp Rupert and banging two pots together in case his vocal volume was insufficient to rouse him.

Laurel sat up, squinting at the bright window. The peddler banged his pots loudly, hollered for Framp again, and then Laurel heard him crawling down from the driver's seat of his wagon and heading toward the house. She heard Framp go to the door and exit. Then, moving to the window with the aid of a single crutch and peeping around the edge of the curtain, she saw both men, Framp in his long underwear, standing out in the yard with no apparent embarrassment. The peddler was talking loudly, but he was so overwrought that his words were slurred and she could not understand him.

Then the peddler began to curse violently, and that she did understand. Framp pushed him, telling him to watch his language because his young niece was in the house and could probably hear everything he said. And his brother-in-law was in there, too, Framp said, and would be out in a moment with his pistol in hand, and at that point the peddler would be in trouble, because Billy Sawyer was a famous pistol fighter who once rode with Bloody Bill Quantrill back during the war.

Laurel had never heard a tale like that about her father. But she had heard of Bloody Bill, and thought him a nightmarish figure. Surely this was another of Uncle Framp's lies; her father would never have associated with such a killer. Would he?

She wondered where Billy was. By now he should be outside, looking out for Framp the way he had when that big fellow named Junior had showed up. She turned, thinking of going to check on her father, and noticed a scrap of paper sticking out from under her pillow. She fetched it. Her name was written on it in her father's handwriting.

Curiosity overwhelmed her, but she was also filled

with a strange dread. Why would her father leave her a note, rather than just tell her whatever he had to say to her face? And where was he, anyway? He couldn't have slept through all that pan-banging and yelling outside.

She opened the note and began to read. Her eyes grew bigger and her heart beat faster at every new word.

Just then the yelling intensified, and she went back to the window. What she saw left her breathless.

The two men were fighting. The pots had been dropped, and Uncle Framp had the peddler trapped, bending him over with the back of the peddler's neck trapped in the crook of Uncle Framp's arm. The peddler was trying hard to get away, struggling and pulling.

Laurel put her hand over her mouth and felt tears start from her eyes. She'd never seen grown men fight before, and it terrified her. But she couldn't tear herself away. Her eyes grew large as she saw the peddler dig into his pocket and come out with a folded-up knife. He tried to open it, but couldn't get positioned to do so.

Laurel froze for several seconds, but when she saw the man finally get the knife open, she broke out of her paralysis. Running out of her little room and through the house as best a crippled girl on a crutch can run, she reached the front door and shoved it open, starting outside.

"Uncle Framp!" she screamed. "He's got a knife! A *knife!*"

And just then the knife cut flesh. The peddler managed to probe the tip of it into Framp's thigh. Framp howled, more in surprise than pain, and began to squeeze harder on his opponent's neck.

But it had no obvious effect, except to make the peddler fight him harder. And it looked to Laurel like he was going to break free any moment. Then, she knew, that knife would go into her uncle's heart, or throat.

Her father had always told her that strength comes to those who need it, when they need it, if they will only let it come to them. With that thought ringing in her mind, she began looking about for a weapon—a stick, a stone, a piece of broken crockery—anything.

She found none of those things, but she did find a weapon. She hefted one of the peddler's dropped pots with her hand not occupied with holding her crutch, aimed, and swung it hard at her moving target—the peddler's exposed head.

She missed, and staggered against the fighting men. Her weight was meager, but sufficient to unbalance both of them. They fell, going down hard, and Laurel landed atop them. The peddler let out a yell, quite sharp, and suddenly Laurel was shoved aside and rolled off onto the ground. One of the figures rose. She turned and saw it was her uncle.

Framp got up clumsily, and staggered away from the fallen peddler. There was a little bit of blood on his thigh, staining his long underwear crimson. Laurel got up and hurried back toward the door. The peddler was still down; he'd struck his head on a tree root as he fell. He wasn't out, though, only momentarily stunned.

Framp took advantage of the moment to step on the peddler's wrist, clamping down the hand that held the knife. Framp stooped quickly and wrenched the knife free.

"Uncle Framp?" Laurel called from the doorway. "Uncle Framp, are you all right?"

"Other than a little cut on my leg, I'm fine, child."

"Who is he, Uncle Framp?"

"A very bad man, Laurel. A thief and murderer."

The peddler got up, cursing, shaking his head clear. "Don't believe that, girl!" he said. "It's *him* who's the thief and murderer! It's him who let my brother go to jail for something *he* did! And my brother *died* there, girl! Died locked up for something he never done, but this bastard did!"

"Don't listen to this liar, Laurel," Framp said. He had the knife in hand now, held with the blade extending down from his fist. He shook it at the peddler. "Keep your mouth shut, Newberry! Shut up or I'll shut you up!"

"You didn't really do that, did you, Uncle Framp?" Laurel asked from the door.

Framp shot a hot glare at her, then looked down at the peddler cringing on the ground below him. He turned and stepped away, walking in Laurel's direction.

Then he stopped abruptly, and grasped at his head. "Good Lord!" he said, staggering backward. "I'm dizzy . . . can't . . . stand . . ."

He turned as he fell, groping outward with his right hand, the hand that held the knife. Laurel gaped in horror as the knife in her uncle's hand drove down toward the supine peddler, who screamed terribly as it drove into his chest, digging deep into his heart. He gurgled and writhed a couple of moments, blood flooding out his chest and running down his side onto the ground. Then he lay still, eyes glazed.

Framp's hand still held the grip of the knife, his arm touching the flowing blood . . . blood that ceased to flow even as Laurel watched, sickened.

Framp got up, letting go of the knife, which remained buried in the peddler's chest. Laurel drew near, then stopped, not wanting to be any closer.

"Is he dead, Uncle Framp?"

"He is, Laurel. Too bad. I didn't want that to happen. Didn't mean for it to. I just got dizzy, fell."

"What made you get dizzy?"

"Being hit on the head by that metal box during the storm. I've been struck by dizziness a few times since then."

"But you reached out the knife, Uncle Framp. You reached out your hand so it came down on him."

"I was just trying to catch myself, Laurel. I didn't even remember I had the knife in my hand."

"It looked ... it looked like you *wanted* to do it, Uncle Framp."

"Not everything is what it looks like, girl. It was an accident, I swear." Framp frowned at her. "I wish you'd not seen it, though. Why'd you come out here, Laurel?"

"I heard the noise, saw you and that man arguing. I thought you might need help."

"So I get help from a little girl, and my own brother-in-law just stays in his bed. Where's your father, Laurel?"

Everything she'd read in that note beneath her pillow came flashing back. Her father was gone ... with the manuscript. With what Framp would consider *his* manuscript.

So she lied, something her father told her was wrong, but in this case she dared not tell the truth. "I don't know where he is, Uncle Framp. Asleep, I guess."

"Hard to believe he could sleep through all that pan-banging and noise."

"Why did that man come here, Uncle Framp? Why did he say those things about you?"

"Because he's an evil man. A liar. He's somebody I knew in the past, somebody I got away from and had nothing to do with after I saw what a devil he really was. I don't know what brought him here today, or how he even knew where to find me. But he's gone now. Thank God he's gone."

"Will you be in trouble, Uncle Framp? Will the law say you did something bad?"

"Not if the law doesn't know what happened." Framp paused and looked at the house. "Laurel, it's good that your pa didn't wake up. It's good he didn't see this. Now I want you to go back in, and don't wake him up, and don't tell him a thing about this if he does wake up. And don't watch me. I've got something I've got to do, to make sure I don't get into trouble, like you said."

"All right, Uncle Framp."

"Thank you for coming out to help me, Laurel. You probably shouldn't have done it, but thank you anyway."

"You're welcome, Uncle Framp. What is it you're going to go do?"

"Just get rid of some things, that's all. Nothing you need to worry about, nor watch."

She went into the house and back to her bed. Only after she lay down did she begin shaking. She trembled like a leaf in wind, unable to stop, and unable to shake from her mind the image of that knife digging into the peddler's heart.

Was Uncle Framp a murderer? Or had it really been only an accident? She wasn't sure, and the uncertainty made her afraid, especially with her father gone.

The note hadn't told her not to tell Framp that Billy

had taken the manuscript, only to claim illness, if necessary, to keep him from following. But why tell him at all?

She answered her own question: because Framp would discover the manuscript was gone, and that Billy Sawyer was gone, and it would not be hard for him to put the two together. Her father surely had realized that, or else he would have told her to keep from Framp the truth of what he'd done.

Laurel heard the creaking of the peddler's wagon driving away. She got up and went to the window, peering out secretively. The body was no longer on the ground, and the wagon was rolling off, Framp in the driver's seat.

He was going to hide the body. What else could he be doing?

And it was then that she felt sure of it: Uncle Framp really had murdered that man . . . or at least deliberately killed him. Was all deliberate killing murder? Laurel didn't know. Maybe Framp had done it because he thought he had to in order to save his own life.

She watched the peddler's wagon ride out of sight over the hill, and her eyes drifted over to the shed from which her father had taken the Farnsworth manuscript. A realization struck her: There might be a way to hide the absence of the manuscript from Framp, so that he'd never know her father had taken it. It would take some daring on her part, but it could work. . . .

And the time had to be now, while Framp was away.

Rising, she steeled herself for what she knew she had to do, and hoped she would not lose courage.

Chapter Nine

Billy Sawyer woke up late in the morning, having slept since dawn. It wasn't much rest for a man who had ridden all night, but he was glad for it, as far as it went.

He sat up and rubbed his eyes, and looked across the little camp to where Junior Gaylord sat up against a tree, mouth hanging open, eyes closed, heavy snores emanating. A crumpled newspaper lay across his lap, held in place by his own limp arm.

Billy got up, yawning, wondering where Junior had found a newspaper. He stretched, looked up at the sun to see how far along the day was, and decided Junior's sleep time was over, too. They needed to get on the move, to get to Dodge while there remained a chance Farnsworth would still be there.

Billy walked over, intending to nudge Junior awake with his foot, but he happened to spot a word in a headline of the rumpled newspaper: *Farnsworth*. Kneeling,

he looked closer, read the headline, then carefully slipped the paper out from under Junior's arm. Billy went back to his bedroll and sat down on it, happy now to let Junior sleep a few more minutes so he could read this story about the very man he was trying to find.

The story, only three days old, was not only about Farnsworth, but also his missing manuscript. The writer had managed to learn, not directly but through things Farnsworth had told others in Dodge saloons and the others had repeated, that the great writer had suffered quite a loss in the recent cyclone that had battered the town of Rockfield, Kansas. The only working manuscript in existence of his new novel, entitled *Mortimer Straw*, had been literally blown away from him when the twister had knocked his wagon off the road while he tried to flee the town right after a lecture delivered in the local library.

There was little news in this to Billy, but the further he read the more providential it seemed that this newspaper had turned up. He wondered if Junior had had this paper with him even before they set out, or if not, how he'd come by it. It was crumpled and dirty; maybe he'd just found it, or it had blown across the landscape.

Providential either way, for as he read, Billy learned that Farnsworth was deeply troubled at the loss of his manuscript. So troubled, the article said, that he was offering a reward of some amount, apparently not yet finally decided, to anyone who could bring the manuscript safely back to him, in its entirety.

Billy closed his eyes and pictured Laurel walking normally, smiling, healthy. It really could happen. No one else would be able to return that manuscript, for no one else had it.

Except Junior. Billy looked at the sleeping man and wished he could cause him to sleep for a month. With Junior out of the picture, Billy could proceed without impediment, locate Farnsworth, and gain that reward.

But he couldn't get rid of Junior. He was no murderer; he couldn't just shoot the man. And even if he broke away from him now, while he slept, Junior knew where Billy was going and would catch up with him shortly, and maybe decide to repay Billy by taking the manuscript for himself.

No, for Laurel's sake, Billy would stay on the course he'd begun. He and Junior would go to Farnsworth, and if Billy was lucky, the reward would be enough to take care of Laurel's needs even after Junior claimed his share. Not that Junior actually deserved a share. Framp had the better claim, having been the actual finder of the manuscript.

Framp, of course, would be furious that Billy had taken the manuscript. And it was inevitable he would discover its absence. That was why Billy had not asked Laurel to hide the fact that the manuscript box was missing. Framp would investigate the shed as soon as he discovered Billy was gone.

The only hope of keeping Framp from following him once he realized the truth was Framp's devotion to Laurel. If she could persuade him she was ill and needed his care, that might keep him from pursuing the manuscript.

Billy went back to his blankets and sat down on them, his mind wandering back to Framp's house and his daughter. *What was happening back there right now?* he wondered. Had Framp yet discovered that the manuscript was gone?

Billy hoped and prayed that Laurel was well, and that

he had done the right thing in leaving her alone with such a volatile fellow as Framp Rupert.

Framp had gone away from the house on the peddler's wagon, but he came back on foot. The dead man's body would not be found. It resided now in the bottom of an old, dry well behind an abandoned farmhouse.

Framp had dumped him down, then dropped in assorted pots, pans, and other goods from the wagon. The old horse that had pulled the wagon was now a free creature, roaming in a pasture where several horses belonging to a neighboring ranch also foraged. Framp knew the rancher, knew especially that he was a scatterbrained fellow. Probably he would never even notice that the number of horses he possessed had just grown by one. The peddler's nag would simply assimilate with the others and become invisible.

The smell of smoke hung strong on Framp's clothing. The wagon had been harder to set afire than he'd anticipated it would be, but finally it had caught, and Framp had watched the flames eat it away until nothing but metal fragments remained. He was relatively sure now that no one would ever notice that the peddler was no longer in the world, and if there was a good rain or two, perhaps even the marks left by the burning of the wagon would wash away.

That's the trouble when you have crime in your background, Framp thought. *There's always some old straggler from the past, mad about something, coming around and trying to settle an old score. Then you got to kill them just to keep them from killing you, or ruining your life.*

Framp didn't regret the killing of the peddler in itself. He regretted only that his innocent niece had to see it and thereby become entangled, if only as a witness.

Framp breathed hard, not accustomed to the level of exertion he had just put forth. Fighting, killing a man, hauling off a body, dumping it down a well, covering it, burning the wagon . . . it was enough to exhaust a man.

And it was darned hard to breathe, anyway. Something about the air . . . something *in* the air. He coughed. Walked farther, coughed some more.

Smoke. That was what hung in the air. Not visible smoke, but thick enough to smell and to coat the throat and upper portions of the lungs.

Hard to believe that peddler's wagon had put so much smoke into the air. And then Framp realized that the wind was blowing from the wrong direction to allow the burned peddler's cart to account for the smoke he smelled. Something else was burning . . . something ahead of him.

Worried now, he hurried. *Don't let it be my house*, he thought urgently. *Don't let it be my house*.

It wasn't his house. It was the shed behind it. Framp stopped in his tracks as soon as his place came into view and gaped at the sight of flames licking up the walls of the shed. Part of the roof was already burned away.

Dear God, how could it have happened? What would cause a fire to break out? Had someone set the place ablaze?

The manuscript. It was hidden in there. Perhaps already burned up by now.

Framp lost his paralysis and ran down the slope toward the house. Where was Laurel? Might she have started the fire somehow? Why would she do so?

He reached the shed, pushed open the door, and

jumped back as fire reached out toward him. He felt the hot brush of it on his face. Smoke and heat stung and momentarily blinded his left eye.

But he was not worried about his eye as he stumbled backward and fell onto his rump. The manuscript. If it was still in that shed, it was almost certainly nothing but ash by this point. The fire was heaviest in the corner of the shed in which the manuscript had been secreted.

A hand touched his shoulder just as his left eye cleared and he could see with it again. He turned. Laurel, with tears in her eyes, was beside him.

"Laurel, what happened?" he asked. "How did the shed catch afire?"

Did she hesitate before she answered? Or was he simply looking for something not there? He wasn't sure.

"It's my fault, Uncle Framp," she said. "I did something I shouldn't have done."

"Did you set the fire, Laurel?"

"Not on purpose, Uncle Framp."

"How, then?"

"I. . . . I did something I shouldn't have done."

"Matches?"

"Yes. I found some in a drawer. And I found a cigar."

"A cigar?" He frowned at her. "You decided to try smoking a cigar?"

"Yes," she said. "I'm sorry. But you were away, and Papa isn't here, and I just wondered what it would taste like."

"Laurel . . . you know that cigars are for men, not for girls."

"I know. I just wanted to know what it tasted like, that's all. I didn't mean to start a fire."

"You said your father is gone . . . where is he?"

111

"I . . . I don't know."

Framp's eyes narrowed. He glared at Laurel, then at the burning shed. "Are you sure you're telling me the truth about how this fire commenced?"

"Why wouldn't I tell you the truth, Uncle Framp?"

"Because it's mighty peculiar that your father disappears, and all at once my shed catches fire."

The front window of the shed shattered suddenly and flames licked out, lapping up toward the roof. Heat struck Framp and Laurel, who scrambled up and back toward the house.

"God, I hope it doesn't spread to the house!" Framp said.

"Uncle Framp, my Papa didn't start that fire, if that's what you think."

"I don't know what I think. But I can tell you, Laurel, that there was something in that shed that was mighty important. Something your father would have liked to have gotten hold of. I'm thinking maybe he did get hold of it. But maybe he didn't want me to know that, so he put fire to my shed, figuring to burn up everything in it. And that way, in his thinking, I'd figure that the thing hid in there was burned up along with everything else, and not realize that he took it."

Laurel's heart hammered fast. Framp had gotten onto her scheme more quickly than she would have guessed, even if he was wrongly attributing it to her father. She didn't know what to say.

"If that was your papa's plan, Laurel, there's one flaw in it. One way I can find out the truth."

Hearing this took from Laurel's legs what minor bit of strength they possessed. What was Uncle Framp talking about? What had she not thought of?

The shed was fully engulfed, the heat hard to endure even up against the rear of the house. Framp, looking nervously at paint peeling from the heat-assaulted wall of his home, grabbed up Laurel as she began to collapse, and dragged her into the house. He shoved her into a chair and stood glaring down at her.

She could not hold back tears. At that moment she was badly scared of her uncle, and wished that her father were there. He would protect her . . . Uncle Framp would not hurt her if Papa were here!

But he wasn't. He was gone with the manuscript. And Uncle Framp seemed to have figured that out.

Framp looked hatefully at his niece. "You know what the flaw in your papa's thinking is, Laurel? Do you?"

"No. I don't know what you mean, Uncle Framp."

"Laurel, that Farnsworth book was out there in the shed. I'd found it. Didn't tell your papa, for that would have ruined my chances to make any kind of good money with them pages. Your papa has this notion that old Farnsworth would be so damned grateful to get his book back that he'd just open up his pockets and dump out a fortune in reward. Maybe he would . . . but I'm betting he'd dump out plenty more if he was given a little gouge."

"You had that book all this time?"

"I found it. Stuck up in a tree in its metal box. Storm blew it right up there."

Laurel knew about the manuscript, of course, but she tried her best to look surprised by all this.

"Your papa has took away my manuscript, Laurel. I believe you knew that already. He found it in the shed, he took it, and he told you to wait until I was away and set the shed afire. That way, the fact that the manuscript was missing would be covered up. I'd just figure it to have burned up in the fire."

"My papa never told me to burn down the shed!" Laurel protested. "He never!"

"Well, then maybe you thunk that part up yourself. Is that it, Laurel? Did you know what your papa had done, and you tried to cover it up by burning the shed?"

That was *exactly* it, but Laurel certainly wasn't going to tell Framp that. So she simply gaped at him, lip trembling and heart hammering.

"Only one problem with that plan, whoever's it was," Framp said. "I'll still be able to tell if that book was in the shed when it burned. If you think about it, you'll know how."

She frowned, thinking. "Oh . . . the box," she said.

"That's right. Because that metal box would pretty much come through the fire, even if the pages in it turned to ashes. So once that shed finishes burning, and the remains cool down, I'm going to dig through the ashes until I find that box . . . or don't find it. If I don't find that box, then I'll know it was took out of the shed before the fire ever started. And with your papa missing, it's a pretty easy guess as to who took it."

"Uncle Framp," Laurel said, "you won't find that box in the ashes."

"Ah! Now the truth begins to come out! Tell me for a fact, girl: What happened here? Did you take the manuscript?"

Laurel tried to remember what her father had instructed her in the note he'd left, but she was too upset, too scared just now, to do anything but tell the truth.

"I didn't take the manuscript, Uncle Framp. But I'm

the one who found it. I saw you through the shed window, looking at it. And I told Papa."

Framp's lip twitched and for a terrifying moment it seemed to Laurel that he was thinking of striking her. She cringed back reflexively.

That only seemed to make him madder. "Why did you do that? You think I'm the kind to hit a little girl? You think I'd hit my sister's own child?"

"No, Uncle Framp. No."

"Huh. Well, you sure didn't mind hitting *me*, did you?"

"I never hit you, Uncle Framp."

"Yes, you did. Right in the heart. You stole from me. You lied to me."

"I didn't steal from you."

"You put my manuscript into your papa's hands. That was stealing."

"It wasn't your manuscript, Uncle Framp. It was Mr. Farnsworth's."

"Your father made it his, though."

"Only to take it back to Mr. Farnsworth." And just as she said it, Laurel sucked in her breath, knowing she'd just done the very thing her father had told her not to do.

"Ah! So now we all know the truth! He did take it!"

"Uncle Framp, please! I wasn't supposed to tell!"

"You done the right thing to tell me. I was the finder of the manuscript. I'm the one who ought to get it back to its owner."

"Don't go after him, Uncle Framp. Please."

"And why not?"

"Because . . . because I'm starting to feel sick. Really sick. I need you to take care of me."

Framp frowned. "The hell . . . he told you to say that

to me, didn't he? He figured I'd stay behind and take care of you while you were 'sick,' and he'd be free to go claim money from Farnsworth. *My* money, rightfully."

"He'll be mad at me when he finds out I told," Laurel said.

"I'll tell him I figured it out on my own," Framp replied. "Or maybe there's a way I can do this that will never let him find out at all."

"How?"

"I'd as soon not say."

"Don't hurt him, Uncle Framp."

"You think I'd hurt anybody?"

"I saw you kill that peddler today."

"An accident, girl. Just an accident."

"Then why did you haul off his body? Did you hide it?"

"Never you mind what happened to that body. You got trouble enough of your own. It ain't legal to set somebody's property afire, you know. I could have you in every kind of trouble if I had a mind to do it."

"I was just trying to keep you from finding out about the book being gone. So my father could get away safe."

"Well, your plan didn't work, child. I do know, and I'm going after him."

"You don't know where he is. I don't even know."

"I know. He was heading for the place Farnsworth was. Dodge. If I head for Dodge, too, I'll find him."

"Then what?"

"Then I'll talk him into partnering up with me. We'll go together to Farnsworth. Get money for our trouble, and come back with it. Then you can go to Chicago, or wherever that doctor is, and get work done on your limbs. And that will be a good thing, eh?"

"Yes," she said. "It would. Just don't hurt my father, Uncle Framp. Promise me."

He took a slow breath. "I promise."

"Good."

Chapter Ten

"What's wrong, Junior? It's making me nervous to watch you. . . . Why are you so interested in what's behind us?"

Billy Sawyer asked the question as he rode at Junior Gaylord's side, still on the long road to Dodge. For the moment, the manuscript was safely tucked into Billy's saddlebag.

"You ever get feelings, Billy Sawyer? Just notions of things that you can't really put a finger on?"

"Sometimes, I guess."

"Well, I got a feeling. A bad one. Trouble out there. Maybe on our tails."

"You seen something? Heard something?"

"No. Just felt it. Silly, I guess."

"I wouldn't say that. I put a good deal of store by intuition. Sometimes we know more than we think we do."

"Intuition. Is that what you call it?"

"It's one name for it."

"It's this book we're carrying. I think there's bad luck tied to it for some reason. Look at all that's happened. First off, old Farnswoggle loses it to a storm. What's the odds of that? And then it comes crashing down onto the noggin of our good friend Frampton. Again, what's the odds?"

"I don't know much about odds, Junior. I guess that box of paper had to land somewhere. And if somebody's out in the open watching a storm blow things around, I figure the odds are a lot better that that person is going to maybe get hit by something or other blowing in the wind. That something just happened to be Farnsworth's book this time."

"Yeah. A book that old Farnsworth has rendered valuable by talking about reward and such."

"That's right. So we need to be careful with it."

"Righto. Very careful."

"You know, Junior, I've been thinking about this while we've been riding. You know how the newspaper is always carrying stories it picks up from other newspapers? You ever noticed that?"

"Matter of fact, yes."

"As famous as Farnsworth is, and as big a subject as that tornado has been these past days, it's a sure bet that a lot of other papers will be printing, or reprinting, I guess you'd say, that story about Farnsworth's reward on the manuscript."

"I'd say you're right, Billy."

"So the word is going to be out there, spread far and wide. And there'd be plenty who would love to get their hands on that manuscript if they could. Maybe more folks than we'd even guess."

"Let's not let it out of our sight, then."

"I agree. And let's vow to be fair with one another, neither of us trying to make this bargain work to our own individual advantage."

"Let's don't cheat each other, in other words."

"Precisely."

"I won't cheat you, Billy. We're partners, you and me."

"Framp is going to say that I cheated him, Junior. I just want you to know that."

"Because you took the manuscript away from him?"

"That's right. But it wasn't his manuscript. That's the key. I was taking back something that belonged to someone else, for purposes of returning it to the rightful owner. Framp wanted to hold it for ransom, rather than reward. A big difference. Can you see that?"

"I see it. But I think Framp just had the idea that when you're milking, you may as well squeeze for all you can get. No point in getting half a bucketful when you can fill up the whole thing."

"True—if the milk is coming from *your* cow, and not being stolen from your neighbor's."

"You're an honorable man, Billy Sawyer. A way better man than me."

"I don't know that I am."

"You are. And a hell of a lot better one than Framp."

Billy paused, then said, "I don't know that I'm inclined to argue with you on that point. Though Framp's got his good side. He cares for my little girl a good deal, and that counts for much."

They rode until the day was waning, and found themselves in an area devoid of much settlement, but rich in streams, leading to more forestation than was typical in this part of Kansas. They made camp when darkness came in a grove of trees on the west bank of a swift and noisy creek. Junior built a fire, boiled coffee, and cooked salty bacon from a supply he kept in his saddlebag. Billy dug into his own supplies and made biscuits in his small Dutch oven. Made them the way he'd seen Framp make them back at his house—Mandy's way. And the results were good. Almost as good as the biscuits Mandy had made years ago.

When they'd eaten and consumed almost all the coffee, they settled back and rested trail-weary bones. Then Junior rose and produced a flask from somewhere, and Billy suddenly found himself sharing Junior's feeling that trouble was near. Probably within that very flask.

Billy could live with the idea of Junior as a partner, as long as Junior behaved himself, but he couldn't stomach the idea of traveling with a drunkard.

"Junior, how much of that you planning on drinking?" he asked.

"I don't know. However much the fancy takes me, I reckon."

"Don't get drunk on me. You'll just slow us down."

"Two swallows. Just enough to settle me."

"All right. I reckon."

Junior was good to his word. But as Billy watched him taking his second swallow, he was surprised to see Junior freeze in place, flask held to his lips.

"Hold on, Junior. That second swallow can't be the entire contents of the flask."

Junior lowered it. "No, that wasn't what I was doing," he said, speaking more quietly than before. "I just saw something that surprised me, that's all. We ain't alone in these woods."

121

Billy followed the direction of Junior's eyes and saw, through the trees, the flicker of firelight. Then the wind shifted a little and all at once he could smell the smoke of the other camp, and a delicious aroma of frying chicken.

"I believe they fared better than us, Junior," Billy said. "We had bacon and they've got chicken."

"Wonder who it is?"

"I don't know. You think they know we're here?"

"I believe that big fell-over dead tree there probably hides our fire from them," Junior observed. "Probably they ain't spotted us."

"Good. Because I'm getting that same bad feeling you talked about earlier."

"Let's go have a look at them," Junior suggested.

"All right. But let's do it quietly. I got no desire to be shot at."

The camp was farther away than Billy had supposed. The initial illusion of its proximity was accounted for by the size of the fire. No mere cookfire, this was a roaring conflagration, a bonfire worthy of a calf roast. The nearer Billy and Junior drew, the more clearly their noses informed them that more than chicken was being cooked here. Pork, beef, pheasant . . . whoever these people were, they were in a feasting frame of mind.

Billy and Junior found an observation point that kept them hidden but provided a good view of the camp. They settled in for observation, both thinking, but not saying, that the bacon and biscuits they'd eaten didn't seem quite so satisfying now.

"What do you reckon?" Junior whispered. "Cattlemen?"

"Probably. Having some sort of celebration, I think."

They watched for ten minutes. Food was heaped on platters, coffee and liquor flowed, and before long both hidden watchers realized they were observing the birthday celebration of some young, wealthy cattleman. Probably one of the celebrated Ames family, who possessed great holdings in these parts.

This party was taking place on the edge of the woods. Out beyond, the plains spread into the thickening darkness until they faded into nothing. Billy was looking out that way when he saw something move, something drawing near to the firelit scene from the flatlands: a wagon, driven by a young fellow in a huge hat, and occupied by several floridly dressed women.

"Billy, I think the nature of this celebration is about to take a new turn," Junior said. "I know some of them women. I can call them women, for they sure ain't ladies."

Junior was right. Before long the scene around the campfire became something out of an ancient fresco showing the debaucheries of the barbarian world. Billy became quite uncomfortable watching it all. Junior had no similar qualms, and giggled like a foul-minded little boy.

Billy was ready to leave, certainly not wanting to be caught in hiding, watching the sorts of things going on in the light of the bonfire. He was no peeping tom. But just as he was about to slip away, he saw more movement on the plains. A rider came in and dismounted.

Billy drew in his breath and held it. The man who'd just dismounted was the same fellow who'd talked to Junior in the Iron Forge Saloon, the Englishman who bore such a striking resemblance to Joe Spradlin. The same Englishman who, as best Billy had surmised it out, was someone Charles Oliver Farnsworth was trying hard to avoid.

"Chastity!" the Englishman shouted. At the same time he reached to the butt of a pistol holstered at his right hip. "Chastity!"

If this fellow was shouting in favor of that particular virtue, it seemed to Billy he'd come to the wrong party.

"What are *you* doing here?" a large woman called out of the fornicating human mass in the camp. She emerged from the mix, struggling back into a bright scarlet dress. The Englishman lunged in her direction.

"Chastity!" he exclaimed. "Chastity, I've come for you."

So *that* was it. Chastity was her name, not her virtue.

"Why'd you come for me?" Chastity demanded. "I ain't yours!"

"That isn't what you told me yesterday, my dear. Perhaps you should refresh your memory."

"You talk funny, mister," hollered a cowboy.

"He's from England," Chastity explained. "He does talk funny. And he's got funny notions, too. He thinks he owns a woman just because he funned himself with her once."

"Once?" the Englishman said. "Don't you mean eight times, Chastity? And only three of those times involving the exchange of money."

"I'll tell you who owns Chastity," said another man. "Whoever handed her the last dollar. She's a whore, Englishman. Nobody owns her."

The authoritative tone and manner of the speaker convinced Billy that this fellow was in charge of this debauched gathering. Perhaps he was one of the Ames sons, who had reputations as hard-drinking, hard-loving young rakes.

"I know you," the Englishman said. "And you're a damned fool to have called attention to yourself, Ames. Your wealth and big name mean nothing to me. She's my woman, not yours!"

"I disagree, you prissy redcoat!"

With no more provocation than that, the Englishman drew out his pistol, leveled it, and shot the younger man through the chest. The victim fell back, grunting, blood bursting out of his chest and also an exit wound in his back. He moved only a moment or two before dying.

Chastity squalled as if the bullet had struck her rather than the young man, and collapsed in a faint.

"Well, that takes care of that bit of difficulty," the Englishman said, holstering his pistol.

"No wonder Farnsworth tries to stay away from that man," Billy whispered to Junior.

Junior's hand gripped Billy's forearm suddenly, so hard that Billy almost yelled. He pulled free and glared at Junior, wondering what had prompted such a strange action.

He was surprised to see Junior's face twisted in bitter anger. His eyes all but blazed. "Did you see that?" he whispered sharply, loudly enough that Billy instinctively signaled him for silence, fearing the Englishman would hear.

But Junior was too wrought up. He moved as if to lunge up and out into the open, toward the murderous Englishman. But Billy managed to grab him around the elbow and pull him back down. Junior thumped to the ground, breaking a stick beneath him and making a good deal of noise.

"What the devil's wrong with you, Junior?" Billy whispered. "You want to get us caught? Maybe shot?"

"Murderer!" Junior wheezed, his voice oddly tight. "Murderer! He killed that Ames boy in the same way my own pappy was murdered . . . shot to death by a jealous man. Shot him dead! God, it makes me mad. Mad!"

"He'll shoot us dead, too, this one will, if he realizes we're hiding here watching him," Billy whispered. "Please, Junior, calm down. And *quiet* down."

Junior was trembling in agitation, but got hold of himself sufficiently to get down low again, well out of sight. And to Billy's pleasure, it appeared the Englishman had not detected them. Billy hunkered low and watched the Englishman through a gap in the brush. The man was preoccupied by the killing he'd just performed, walking over and looking down at the body of Ames.

Chastity, having recovered from her collapse, approached the Englishman. Billy tensed, anticipating that she would attack him, retaliate for the murder. At the same time she moved, Junior moved as well, creeping back into the trees as if to leave this place. Billy didn't fault that idea at all, but feared that Junior would make noise and attract attention.

The woman reached toward the Englishman. Billy waited for the flash of a knife or the firing of another shot, perhaps from some hidden Derringer she carried.

Apparently she carried no weapons, though. Nor was she intent on punishing the man. She touched his shoulder gently, a soft caress. He turned to her, tense at first, then relaxing. He embraced her, standing above the man he'd just killed, a man who had only minutes before been involved in the most intimate way with her.

It's a foul and evil world we live in, Billy thought.

The woman and the Englishman talked, speaking too low for Billy to hear. The others present slowly drifted off, escaping, some into the woods, others out onto the plains.

But one man did not flee. He moved behind a tree, then emerged again with a pistol drawn. In reflex, Billy almost shouted a warning, but caught himself. The Englishman saw the fellow anyway, on his own, and drew his own pistol. But the man behind the tree fired first. His show went wild, though, missing the Englishman widely. Billy heard the shot rip through the trees near him.

The Englishman fired quickly, and his shot was true. The man behind the tree tried to duck back for cover, but bullets move faster than men, and he took the shot in the right side of his chest. The force threw him back hard and blood appeared on his torso.

Billy felt a sudden desire to be away from here. Taking Junior's lead from shortly before, he turned and slipped back the way he had come. He found Junior standing there, leaning against a tree, staring out across the plains.

"Junior?" Billy said. "Let's get away from here."

Junior made a strange sighing noise, and began to slowly slip down the tree, shoulder blades abraded by bark. He was nearly on the ground before Billy noticed the clean little hole between his eyes.

The bullet that had missed the Englishman had not missed Junior Gaylord. Billy gaped, finding it hard to believe that his "partner" was so suddenly gone, so dead.

127

"I'm sorry, Junior," Billy said. "I can't do right by your remains. I got to go, as you know. I just got to leave you here. Rest in peace, partner. Rest in peace."

And he moved on.

Chapter Eleven

The figure that emerged from the woods caused Billy to jump to his feet. No question that he intended him harm. Why else would his face be shrouded in a flour-sack mask, with a raised shotgun in his hands?

Billy looked over to where his gunbelt lay on the ground beneath a tree. He could not possibly reach it. He looked back at the intruder, who motioned with the shotgun, indicating he should move toward a sapling to his left. Billy did not dare disobey.

At the tree, he leaned his back against it and took a good look at the intruder. Something about the man attracted his eye and also sparked an inexplicable sense of familiarity. Perhaps it was the gait, the stance. Certainly not the voice. The man hadn't spoken.

"What do you want from me?" Billy asked, hoping to prompt a reply.

He got nothing but a grunt. Yet the sound of it only

increased that feeling of familiarity. He started to ask a new question, but was stopped when the man grasped his left wrist and yanked it around behind the tree. Then the man shifted, grabbed his right wrist, and pulled it back as well. A moment later rope encircled his wrists and he was bound.

The man came around the tree, holding the shotgun. Billy realized that the fellow must have put it down to tie him. He'd missed an opportunity at that point to rescue himself. If he'd turned quickly enough he might have been able to overpower the momentarily disarmed fellow.

"Who are you and what do you want?" Billy demanded. The man turned his head and glanced back at him through the holes in his sack mask, holes too shadowed to allow Billy to see inside.

The man headed straight for Billy's saddlebags. Billy watched with his breath caught in his throat as the man yanked open one bag, made another grunting sound, this one with an angry overtone, then opened the second. He looked inside, froze for a moment, then pulled out the brazen manuscript box.

Billy's heart sank. He'd hoped that maybe this was merely a random robbery, money the goal. Obviously this was not the case. This robber had come for the manuscript.

"Farnsworth!" Billy called out, wondering if that seemingly unlikely scenario might actually be playing out here. Maybe Farnsworth had somehow learned who had the manuscript, and where it was.

But no. There were too many barriers to plausibility. The man in the sack mask didn't have the build of Charles Oliver Farnsworth. And though he was covered from head to toe, his hands being the only visible flesh presented, Billy had the strong impression that this was a younger man than Farnsworth.

But as he called out the name, the man started and looked at Billy. Clearly he was fighting an impulse to reply. Billy could see it in his posture, his tense stiffness of manner. But the man didn't speak. Billy wondered why.

He tugged at the bonds around his wrists. Quite tight. The ropes bit into his flesh. A moment of panic came. In moments the thief would disappear with the manuscript, taking with him any hope Billy had of Farnsworth's reward. But even worse, Billy would be left here, helplessly tied to a sapling, unable to move. He might not be found for days. Dear God, if the very worst happened, he might not be found until after he'd starved to death, or died of thirst!

Surely not. Surely *someone* would come. But what if? What if? He'd seen unlikely things happen already . . . a storm throwing the manuscript box from the sky right against Framp's skull, Junior Gaylord being shot to death by a stray bullet . . . even this theft, by a silent, masked stranger who seemed so familiar. In Billy Sawyer's world these days, it seemed anything could happen.

The thief headed away, vanishing into the trees. Billy swallowed his pride and called after him.

"Wait! Don't leave me here . . . I might not be able to get loose."

No reply. He called out again. Nothing. But he did imagine that he heard the man change course, veer back, not coming into the clearing again, but around through the trees to Billy's side. Then he was behind

Billy . . . and something touched the bonds around his wrists.

Was the man untying him? If so, why?

Dear God . . . what if the man wanted a more permanent solution to the Billy Sawyer problem? He might free him only to shoot him.

But the man didn't free him. He merely loosened the bonds a little, giving them a very slight amount of play. Enough that over time, a very long time, Billy should be able to work his hands free.

Whoever this stranger was, at least he had some degree of mercy in his soul. He was giving Billy a chance to live.

But he was taking away from him the only good hope he'd had in years of giving Laurel the gift of strong, healthy legs. That made him Billy's enemy.

Billy'd work free of his bonds as fast as he could, even if he had to peel half the hide off his wrists and hands to do it. Then he'd track this devil down, get back that manuscript, and get back on course to Farnsworth.

Billy tugged at his bonds, trying to determine how long it would take to get free. As he pulled, he winced; it hurt badly in skin, muscle, and bone. Still he kept on struggling, working his way closer to freedom.

Framp Rupert went to his hidden horse, put the manuscript box into his own saddlebag, and mounted up. His heart was trying to thump its way out of his chest and his breathing was fast. He could hardly fathom that he'd done it. He'd gotten back the manuscript, and without being identified by Billy! If Billy had recognized him, he'd have spoken up. Framp knew Billy well enough to be sure of that.

So the advantage was his. Fate was on Framp's side for once. He had the manuscript and no one else in the world knew it. He could find Farnsworth at his leisure and play it all out from there.

He hoped Farnsworth was still at Dodge, for that was the only lead he had to guide him. If Farnsworth had taken off somewhere, he might prove hard to find. Then again, how well could so famous a man conceal himself? Farnsworth didn't travel randomly. He followed a schedule, a publicized one. Framp felt reassured. He would be able to track Farnsworth easily even if he'd moved on from Dodge to the next place, wherever that may be.

Framp rode. He thought about Billy, tied up to that sapling, and wondered if he would be all right. He'd get free eventually, but what if some wild carnivore got hold of him before "eventually" came? Framp didn't want to be responsible for Billy's death. He'd never be able to look little Laurel in the eye again if that happened.

But he couldn't look himself in the eye if he let this opportunity for gain slip away. What Farnsworth was willing to offer in reward he would probably be willing to quadruple, or better, in the form of ransom. So Framp threw his chin up and out, settled into the saddle, and rode with the confidence of a man who has made a firm choice and is comfortable in the decision.

The feelings inside didn't fully match the outer appearance, though. Still he went on, hoping Billy was at least starting to get himself free . . . and that any dangerous varmints were keeping their distance from him.

But he hoped Billy wasn't too close to freedom. Even though he couldn't know that the man who robbed him was his own former brother-in-law, he'd follow anyway. Follow no matter who he thought the thief was. And to follow, all he'd have to do would be to take the road to Dodge. As best Framp could figure it, the manuscript was valueless to anyone except Farnsworth. Therefore, wherever Farnsworth was, there the manuscript and whoever possessed it, or wished to, would naturally be drawn.

The more distance Framp put between himself and the tied-up Billy Sawyer, the better and freer he felt, and the more confident that *this* time, things were going his way.

It merited some celebration, by gum! He'd find himself a good hotel and spend the night on a comfortable bed, but between now and bedtime, he'd have himself a few good drinks. More than a few. He was going to be a rich man soon.

Time to get good and drunk.

The hotel room was going to cost Framp more than he'd hoped it would, but he took it just the same, reminding himself that, before long, such nickel-and-dime concerns would no longer matter. He put his horse in the livery, his few goods and the manuscript box in his hotel room, and headed out for the saloon across the street. It was called the Bull Run. That was a name Framp would remember easily. What he couldn't remember at the moment, though, was the name of the little town itself. Not that the name mattered. It had a hotel, a saloon, and whiskey. All Framp Rupert needed.

Three hours after he entered the saloon, all the good righteous folk of this unknown hamlet were in their beds, sleeping toward the morning. The unrighteous folk, Framp included, were otherwise occupied. He was still in the saloon, so drunk he'd lost control of his dexterity, having by now dropped and broken one whiskey bottle and three shot glasses. He couldn't remember how many glasses he'd drained. And he was still going. He'd be drunk enough to suit him when he was so far gone he could only drag himself back to his room and bed.

Framp was in a quiet mood, not wanting to talk, but there were some cowboys present, nearly as drunk as he, who were talkative. Their conversation was ostensibly between themselves, but was so loud and intrusive that others were drawn in.

"Never a stroke of luck in my life!" one of the louder drunks wailed. He'd been ranting for an hour about his many misfortunes and inability to make a dollar. In what little part of his brain that remained able to think, Framp wondered how this fellow, if he were as poor as he claimed, was able even to afford the whiskey he was slugging down so freely.

More drinking, more time and talk, and the complainer became a whiner. His slurred voice tightened with emotion and he began to weep aloud. It grated Framp's nerves to hear it.

"If only I could just have a *chance* to make some money!" the complainer sobbed. "If only I could have a shot at it. Why shouldn't I?"

Framp decided to leave, but the fellow quieted down for a spell, so he lingered around to drink some more. Somewhere along the way he crossed a line, and the barroom around him became a blur of smeared colors. The sounds he heard also blended and blurred. Voices spoke words he couldn't quite make out.

He might have passed out for a few moments, because he became aware of something cool and damp against his left cheek. He opened his eyes and found himself staring across the flat surface of the table, looking into an overturned shot glass. The wet on his face was spilled whiskey. He'd obviously lost consciousness, dropped his head forward onto the table, and overturned his glass.

He sat up and was greeted by the whining voice of the same complainer, still ranting about his lack of good fortune and his wish for wealth. Annoyance exploded inside Framp, and he came to his feet, lost his balance and staggered three or four yards, then steadied himself against a beam that ran from floor to ceiling.

"Had a bit too much, have you, friend?" a companion of the whiner asked him.

"You tell your friend he need to quit his mouthing off," Framp said, his words quite slurred. "I'm tired of hearing it. He needs to find a way to make his own fortune, not just whine about it. There's money to be made in all kinds of ways."

The man seemed to find Framp's lecture amusing. "I reckon you must be a rich man yourself, if you've got such a strong notion that money can be so easy found."

"I ain't rich. But I will be, or nearly rich, anyway, right soon."

"How so?"

Something in Framp told him he should restrain his words, but the liquor spoke louder, and he heard himself say, "You ever heard of Charles Oliver Farnsworth?"

"The book-writer fellow? Of course I've heard of him. I've heard of Charles Dickens and Willie Shakespeare, too." The man paused and glanced at his companions. "Which one are *you*, then?"

"I ain't none of them. But I got a book wrote by Farnsworth, and I'm taking it to him so he can reward me for it."

"You know, I've got a book of his, too. Three of them, in fact. If I took them to him, you think he'd reward me, too?"

One of the others present chimed in. "Hold up, Jess. I think I know what this fellow is talking about. Ain't you read in the papers about Farnsworth losing his only copy of his next book in that storm that hit up at Rockfield?"

"No, I ain't."

"Well, he lost it, sure did. I seen stories about it in three, four different papers. He's lost it, and is offering reward money for anybody who can find it and bring it to him. Is that what you're talking about, friend? Have you found his lost pages?"

Framp could not restrain himself. The liquor had taken away common sense and prudence. "Yep. I got it. It was blowed into a tree and stuck there. Right behind my own house."

"You're lying," the man said. "If you've got them pages, why ain't you found him already and collected your reward?"

"He moves around. I'm on my way to him now. He left Rockfield and went to Dodge. I'm taking him his book and I'll find him there, and get my money."

The man who'd been whining about his bad fortunes positioned himself in front of Framp and said, "If I had them pages, I'd not turn it in for reward. I'd tell him he had to pay me more than he was offering for reward. And I'll bet he'd do it."

"I think the same way, mister," Framp replied. "He'll pay me dear, not just some little penny or two out of his pocket, before he gets them pages back again."

"You're a fortunate man, sir," the former whiner said. "It's just such an opportunity I've wished I could find for myself." He paused cunningly, though Framp was too drunk to notice it. "Let me buy you another round, friend. It appears your bottle is empty."

"I don't know that I want no more whiskey," Framp said.

"All right, then. I'll fetch you a beer."

Liquor on beer, never fear. Beer on liquor, never sicker. The familiar little rhyme passed through Framp's mind, but he was too drunk to pay heed to it. "Beer sounds good," he said.

The man fetched the beer. Framp drank it too fast, but took a second one slower. The drunker he grew, the less the other man seemed like the off-putting complainer he'd been before, and the more like a new friend.

Framp was only vaguely aware of it when the man took his arm and led him out of the saloon and across the street. He managed to somehow convey to the man where his room was, and together they climbed the stairs, both of them drunk, Framp the more so.

Framp fumbled out his key, dropped it, actually retrieved it himself, but couldn't find the keyhole. Then he did, and managed to open the door.

His memories of the moments immediately thereafter would be vague, unclear. He recalled pulling off a boot, peeling off his shirt, and falling into the bed. Then it all became even more dreamlike. He lay staring at the metal box containing Farnsworth's manuscript.

He'd left it on a table in the corner before heading out for the saloon.

The other man walked over, examined the box, opened it, studied some of the papers inside.

Framp sat up. "Leave that alone," he tried to say, but what came out was mere nonsensical noise. The other man stared at him a moment, then headed for the door with the manuscript box in hand.

Framp pushed himself out of bed, intent on following, but his feet had no feeling and his legs no strength. He collapsed, a crumpled heap of intoxicated human flesh, and moaned helplessly as a stranger carried away the only hope for significant money that he'd had in his life.

He cursed, cried, slapped at the floor, amazing himself by actually missing it. How could a man be so drunk he couldn't even hit the floor with his own fist? But he'd somehow done it.

Framp stretched out across the floor, his mind a fuzzy, dark fog, and was conscious of nothing else until morning.

Chapter Twelve

Jim Barker was one of those young men of eighteen who looked all of fourteen years old. He'd never much minded his boyish appearance until earlier this year, when he'd fallen hard in love with Mattie Taylor, daughter of the local hardware merchant. Mattie had rebuffed him, treating him like the boy he appeared to be instead of the man he felt he was. Ever since then he'd cursed his smooth, virtually whiskerless face, his slightly high voice, his slender build and delicate, youthful hands. He spent every morning here at his family's cafe, serving meals to customers while mentally dwelling on his shortcomings and dreaming of romantic encounters with Mattie Taylor that would never be.

His mind wasn't so engaged this morning, though. This morning he had a distraction, in the form of a most intriguing customer. The man had entered half an hour before, ordered eggs and ham and biscuits and coffee. When Jim heard his voice, he instantly grew curious about the man. One didn't hear British accents very often here on the Kansas plains.

Jim's mind had gone to work on the mystery, and he'd developed a theory about this man, something surmised based on things he'd been reading lately in the newspapers customers sometimes left lying on the cafe tables.

Gathering up his courage and determined to put his theory to the test, Jim took the coffeepot off the iron stove in the back of the cafe and headed for the Englishman's table. The man had finished his breakfast save for one jelly-laden biscuit, which he was working on very slowly, with coffee.

"More coffee, sir?" Jim asked.

"Indeed, young man," the Englishman replied, holding up his cup. Jim poured it full.

"I thank you, young man."

"My pleasure, sir." Jim paused, then said, "Sir, might I be so bold as to ask you a question? I hope you won't think me rude."

"My curiosity compels me to grant you permission," the Englishman said.

"Very well. Sir, am I right that you are Charles Oliver Farnsworth?"

The man gave Jim an odd look. "Why would you think that?"

"Because you are British, sir. And because I know that Mr. Farnsworth, a writer I much admire, is in the midst of a tour of libraries here on the plains. So I simply put two and two together."

The man smiled, but it was a cold smile. "This time, I fear, you miscalculated your sum. With great pride I tell you that I am not Farnsworth. I am a far better man

141

than he. But I take no offense at your question because I know it derives from your appreciation of his literature. If you only could know it, your admiration for him pays an indirect compliment to me."

Jim was puzzled by the convoluted response, and merely nodded. Something about this man was arrogant and off-putting. He was glad that this wasn't Farnsworth, because he liked Farnsworth's work and wouldn't want to perceive him as being like this fellow.

"Can I get you anything further?" Jim asked, slipping back into his waiter role. As he spoke, he glanced up and out the window, and saw a big woman in a bright red velvety dress striding across the street toward the cafe. She was no beauty, but she was striking—an eye-catcher if only for her gaudy adornment. Jim was young and had no experience with "soiled doves," as most euphemistically called prostitutes, but he was savvy enough to know one when he saw one. He wasn't glad to see her coming toward the cafe. Jim's father, a local deacon of note, deplored it when the dregs of the social order saw fit to patronize his establishment.

The Englishman noticed Jim's attention to the street beyond the window, and looked out through the glass himself. He tensed and cursed beneath his breath, but not far enough beneath it to keep Jim from hearing, nor the only other diner in the place, who just happened to be the wife of the local Methodist minister. She blanched and gasped loudly when she overheard the obscenity the Englishman had muttered, and Jim grimaced, knowing that this would all come back around to him at some point. Wife would tell preacher, preacher would tell Jim's father, and Jim's father would tell him, and somehow manage to make it sound like it was all Jim's fault that the moral climate of the Hot Skillet Cafe had been allowed to decline this morning.

"Merciful God, can a man have no peace?" the Englishman muttered.

"I'm sorry, sir. I didn't mean to pester you," Jim replied.

"No, young man, no. Not you. Her. That woman. Named, of all things, Chastity. No worse case of misnaming has ever been done. She should have been named Glue. She sticks to me like stench to a goat, after all. But Chastity? Her chastity vanished many years ago, and will never be seen again, of that I'm sure."

"I can, perhaps, persuade her not to come in," Jim suggested, though he wasn't sure how he'd do that, or why he should even care to help out this rather harsh man. Especially since he wasn't the famous Farnsworth after all.

"Let her in. If you don't she'll merely grow fretful and find me later on any account. That, young man, is the kind of woman you should shun in life, if you'll take advice from a stranger. I made the mistake of growing to care for her, only to find her in the act of dalliance with another man . . . in return for money. The very whore of Babylon, she is!"

"Sir, she sees you," Jim said.

The woman had reached the boardwalk outside the cafe, and now stood upon it, staring through the window at the Englishman. He looked back at her and she turned and headed for the door.

The door opened and she was in, sweeping back to where her beloved sat glowering. "Ulysses!" she declared, revealing the Englishman's name. "You vanished on me . . . I went to the privy and came back to the room to find you gone."

"Am I supposed to linger around and wait for you every time you vanish?" Ulysses replied.

"I would think that you would want to be sure to keep up with me, after all you did to get me back. For God's sake, Ulysses, you killed a man over me!"

Jim was unable to squelch a gasp. The Englishman frowned up at him briefly.

"I killed a man because he insulted me and threatened me," Ulysses replied. "Don't flatter yourself beyond your due, woman."

"He didn't threaten you, Ulysses. I was there . . . I know what was said and what wasn't said. He did insult you, but he didn't threaten you."

"Don't dispute with me, woman."

"Call me by my name, Ulysses. I'm not 'woman.'"

"You certainly have more 'woman' about you than 'chastity.' I can hardly bring myself to call a whore 'Chastity' without bursting into laughter."

She began to cry, putting her face into her hands. Ulysses rolled his eyes, looked at Jim, and shook his head.

"You have no respect for me, Ulysses," she said.

"I do not. But I'm honest enough to admit it. But this I will tell you, my dear: After my first night with you, I thought myself a man in love. Quite sincerely."

She stopped crying and looked at him in astonishment. "Do you mean that, Ulysses?"

"I do. Why do you think I bothered to intervene when I saw you in the embrace of that young man?"

"Oh, Ulysses Church . . . bless you, darling! You *do* care for me! You *do*!"

"Use the past tense, my dear. I *did* care for you . . . perhaps for fifteen minutes. That has passed."

She blubbered, stammered, and didn't manage to get anything out.

"Are you speaking, whore, or just grunting? Or do you grunt only when you're plying your trade?"

She seemed about to cry again. Jim stepped back, wondering why he was making himself audience to this disgusting exchange. Yet it intrigued and held him, if only because it was a window into a kind of world that was unfamiliar to a sheltered, small-town Kansas boy.

"Ulysses," she said, "would you love me again if I told you something about the manuscript you're trying to find?"

The Englishman's manner changed immediately. He grew deadly serious, so much so that he suddenly seemed dangerous. Jim took another half step back.

"Sit down, whore . . . I mean, please have a seat, Chastity," Ulysses said. "Tell me what you know."

To justify his lingering about, Jim refilled the coffee cup again. He was intrigued by the woman's talk of a manuscript . . . manuscripts went with writers. Might this fellow be Farnsworth after all, traveling under a false name?

"I talked to a man this morning, out there on the street . . ." she began.

"Hardly a new experience for you, eh? Talking to men on the street. You've talked to plenty of them, and done much more than talk."

"Please, Ulysses, don't mock me. I have something important to tell you."

"Talk, then."

"The man I talked to told me there was a man in town last night who claimed he has the manuscript."

145

Ulysses Church reached over and grasped her wrist. It looked initially like a gentle grasp, but Jim watched his fingers tighten. The Englishman's eyes narrowed and she tried to pull away, but he held her fast. "Talk," he said, almost spitting the word.

Jim heard himself cutting in. "It's true," he said. "I heard the same story."

"What do you know? Both of you!" demanded Ulysses.

Chastity stammered out more noise, again nothing sensible. Ulysses swore and said something else about grunting, then turned attention to Jim in hopes of something better.

"Talk to me, young man."

"Well, sir, you know how the newspaper has been saying that Charles Farnsworth lost an unfinished manuscript in that storm up in Rockfield. . . ."

"I know about that, young man. Tell me about the manuscript being in this town."

"Well, the story I heard, from a man in here right after we opened up, was that he was in the saloon last night, and there was a man there who said he had found the manuscript. Said he was taking it to give to Farnsworth in exchange for reward, or ransom, or something."

"Where is this man?"

"I don't know . . . but I think he's staying in the hotel. The man this morning said that he was. One of the man's friends had to walk the man back to his hotel room because he was too drunk to make it alone."

"The hotel yonder? Across the street?"

"That's the only one in town."

"Same hotel I'm in. And my manuscript is there!"

The Englishman smiled . . . Jim thought the smile made him look wicked. "Damn! Can you believe the ironies of fate?"

"Sir, my father owns this cafe, and he doesn't allow cursing in it."

"Damn it, young man, I've lived a difficult life in my native England, crossed a vast ocean to come to this country, where I've found little but strife and thievery and harm. I've lived more than five decades and I am not one to care what some small-town cafe operator thinks about my choice of language."

"Perhaps I shouldn't have spoken." Then Jim looked up and out the window, and froze.

There was a man coming down the exterior hotel steps, which ran from the second floor on the side of the building. He was very disheveled and walked uncertainly, seeming to keep himself on his feet, as he descended the stairs gingerly, by gripping hard on the handrail.

Ulysses followed Jim's gaze. "That's *him*, isn't it! That's the man with my manuscript!"

"*Your* manuscript . . . that's the second time you've said that . . . you *are* Charles Farnsworth!"

"Tell me, boy, is that the man?"

"I don't know," Jim said honestly. "I didn't see him myself. I just heard the story. But that man is in the hotel, and he's a stranger, and he looks like he might have had a few too many drinks last night. . . ."

"So he does, young fellow. So he does. And by the by, I am not Charles Farnsworth. Of course, neither is Farnsworth himself."

"What does that mean?"

"Just consider it a cryptic comment from a visiting

147

fool of an Englishman," he said. "Something to ponder at your leisure."

"Can I get you another biscuit, more coffee, anything else?"

"Hell, no, boy. I've had quite enough of everything. Quite enough of this cafe, this town, this food . . . enough of you, and enough of this whore. On to better things."

Chastity lowered her face nearly to the tabletop and wept. Then she got up, still crying, and fled the cafe through the front door, heading down the street. Jim could see her until she rounded a corner and disappeared.

"Good riddance," muttered Ulysses Church.

Jim turned away and walked back to the rear of the cafe, ready for this strange man to disappear.

Ulysses Church. Just who was he? Why was he here in the American West, pursuing a manuscript written by another man?

Or was it another man? Jim vowed to himself that the next time he saw a portrait of the famed Charles Oliver Farnsworth, he would study it closely, compare the features with those of Ulysses Church. Just to see. Just to be sure.

Framp Rupert staggered, lost his footing, and, out of pure reflex, saved himself from falling down the stairs only by grabbing the railing. He swung his weight onto his hands, pulled his feet back in place beneath him again, and looked up, groaning in pain as sunlight hammered his sensitive eyes. His head throbbed and he felt sick.

And decided right then that it just wasn't worth it.

Not at all. The day held no attraction worth the misery of trying to walk with his head in a vise of pain, trying to see with eyes that hurt every time they took in light, and putting his weight down on feet that felt as formless as hot jelly.

The day could wait. Framp Rupert was going back up the stairs, back into his room, back into his bed. Sure, he'd lost the manuscript, and sure, he might be able to track down the thief if he got an early start . . . but all that presumed the ability to function like a normal man. And he was far too hungover to be a normal man just yet.

Framp, holding the rail for balance, turned and began dragging himself back up the stairs. With his back to the street, he did not see the big man who emerged from the cafe, stared at him, then stepped off the boardwalk to head across to the hotel.

Framp made it to the top of the stairs, paused there a few moments, gasping for air and closing his eyes almost entirely to block out the unwelcome day. Then he went back into the hotel, welcoming the darkness of the hallway, and shuffled down the hall to his room.

He did not hear the voice of the man outside, now on the base of the stairs, calling up to him in a decidedly British accent: "Sir! Sir! Wait . . . let me speak to you!"

The mere noise of the door opening caused Framp's head to throb even worse. He staggered into the room and fell onto the bed, wishing he'd not gotten so drunk the prior night. If he'd stayed sober he'd not feel the way he did now, nor would he have lost the manuscript. Incredible to think that the fellow had been able to merely pick it up and carry it out of the room, with Framp right there. And now it was gone, and so was

Framp's hope of fortune, unless he could track the scoundrel down.

Framp ached too much to sleep, but the bed felt delightful. He writhed a little, settling his body into just the right places, and twisted his head in an attempt to find a position that minimized his pounding headache. As he did this he happened to notice that he'd left the door ajar. He could see right out into the hall.

Didn't matter. If someone happened to catch a glimpse of him collapsed in his bed, what did it matter? He was clothed, and he had a right to be here. And he had nothing left worth stealing, not now that the manuscript was gone.

He had almost managed to drift back to sleep when he heard the door at the end of the hallway, the one leading out onto the stair landing, open and close. There was a movement of shadow on the floor of the hallway outside; he saw it through his room's open door. Then a figure loomed there, looking into his room, staring at him.

If the fellow had walked on past, Framp would have thought little of it. But the man lingered, staring at Framp, who grew steadily more uncomfortable under the scrutiny. Then, when the man stepped into the doorway, pushed the door farther open, and entered the room, Framp sat up, sending a shivering throb of pain from the top of his skull down through his shoulders.

"What do you want, mister?" he managed to ask, though his tongue felt thick as his wrist, and covered with cotton.

"I've lost something and think perhaps it might be in here," the man replied. His accent, Framp noticed, was

British. Good Lord, could this actually be Farnsworth? How many Englishmen could there be roaming through these parts at any given time?

"What did you lose?" Framp asked, sitting upright and propping himself against the headboard. Heaven above, but he hurt! All over.

The intruder ignored the question and posed one of his own. "Are you ill, sir?"

"In a way. Too much to drink last night. Way too much."

"Ah! So you were in the saloon, then."

"I was."

"Are you the gentleman who declared that he had the celebrated lost manuscript of Charles Oliver Farnsworth, and was delivering it back to its rightful owner?"

"How'd you hear about that?"

"Small town. People talk, share stories, tell what they heard in the local drinkery."

"Why should I answer you? Who are you? Are you Farnsworth?"

The man stepped farther into the room and eased the door closed. Framp winced at the sound of it clicking closed. But the man's elegant voice was strangely soothing. "Let us just say that I am an associate of Mr. Farnsworth. I'm seeking to collect the manuscript on his behalf."

"Are you authorized to pay for it? He's offered a reward."

"I'm authorized to do what it requires to get it back. That manuscript is worth a literal fortune to its author. It must be found, must be returned."

"Well, that was my intent, sir. Indeed I did have the

manuscript. Found it in a tree, if you can believe that. Storm lodged it there, and after that it literally fell out of the sky and clunked me on the head."

"Amazing."

"Yes. And it made me figure that was a sign it was intended for me to be the one to return it to Mr. Farnsworth. For the right price, of course. After all, it is a valuable item, and I've gone to some trouble to seek out a way to get it back to its author."

"I'm sure you have. Tell me: Where is it?"

Framp's throat grew tight and his voice could not be found.

He looked in despair at the intruder. The man glared back at him, then advanced.

Chapter Thirteen

"I asked you a question, sir!" the Englishman bellowed. Then his hand drew back.

The first blow was a flat-handed slap. It jarred Framp's skull intolerably, making him feel sick to the pit of his stomach. But his whiskers softened the sting of fingers on flesh, at least.

Framp tried to sit up, but his tormentor shoved him down and leaned across his chest, bearing down weight. Framp did not have the strength to fight him, but the man's head was near enough to his that an inspiration came. Framp lunged his head up, teeth snapping, and managed to hook the Englishman's right earlobe. When he pulled back down again, the lobe was between his teeth and no longer attached to its owner.

Framp spat the gruesome trophy out; it arced upward, cleared the side of the bed, and landed on the floor. The Englishman, groping the side of his head and howling in pain, moved up off of Framp and staggered about, stepping on the earlobe in the process. The little bit of blood that came out of it slickened the floor enough to make him slip, and he landed on his rump.

Despite his terrible condition, Framp knew he had to fight. This man frightened him. Framp got up and tried to punch the man where he sat on the floor, but Ulysses was not impaired as Framp was by being hungover, and dodged the blow easily. He kicked from his seated position and caught Framp just behind the left knee, making it buckle. Framp fell hard onto his knees, and the Englishman struck him twice on the side of his jaw with a fist. Framp flopped over, groaning, and Ulysses came to his feet and pressed a foot into the small of Framp's back, bearing down hard.

"Where is my manuscript?" he demanded again. "Talk, or I'll hammer my boot heel into your spine so hard you'll never walk again!"

"I ain't got it no more!" Framp wheezed out. "It was took from me!"

"How the hell did that happen, and who took it?"

"It was a stranger, a man from the saloon. I was drunk and he walked me up to make sure I could get to my room and into bed, and he took the manuscript. It was lying right over yonder, in a brass box."

"Where did he go?"

"I don't know. Out the door."

"Not a good answer." This blow was harder than any of the prior ones, rattling Framp's teeth and knocking him nearly unconscious.

When he regained his senses, he was in a chair in the corner of the room, tied up with his own galluses. The

Englishman was pacing before him, anger pouring off him like a nearly visible steam.

"Tell me your story, you miserable thief of a man's artistic creation," Ulysses demanded. "Tell me who you are, and every detail of how you came to have that manuscript."

Sensing that this madman would kill him if he didn't cooperate, Framp decided to do just what he was asked. He began to talk, as best his tight and scratchy throat would allow him, and truthfully related the entire story of how the manuscript had come into his life and ultimately into his temporary possession. He told of Billy and Laurel Sawyer, the storm that had taken the manuscript into the sky and tossed it down again, how he'd been struck by it, then found it later in a tree, and of his theft of the manuscript from Billy, and how he'd left him tied to a tree. To his surprise, the Englishman seemed interested in it all and did not try to hurry him or make him skip over details.

When he was done at last, the Englishman looked at him through slitted eyes. "The general thrust of what you've told me—a story too detailed for me to believe it is a contrivance—is that you are not useful to me. You no longer possess the manuscript, nor do you know who does. But you do know my face, and for reasons I am under no obligation to explain to you, that makes you a danger to me."

"I'm no danger to you, sir. You leave me in peace and you'll never hear from me again, nor see me. And I'll tell no one of any of this."

"I will indeed leave you in peace. A gentle, continuing repose."

The Englishman pulled out a small pistol and leveled it on Framp. Then he went over and loosened his bonds. Framp rose, rubbing his wrists, his paled hands regaining color as blood flowed into them again.

"You're letting me go?"

"I'm setting you free to fly like a bird."

"You've got a poetic and pretty way of speaking, mister. But you use your fists like a son of a bitch."

"Walk out into the hallway. Don't run. Remember that I have this gun."

"Whatever you say, mister." Framp did as he was told.

Ulysses directed him out onto the landing of the outdoor stairs. There he ordered Framp to hold still, which he did.

Ulysses joined Framp out on the landing, and squinted toward the window of the Hot Skillet Cafe, in which he'd had his breakfast. "Do you see anyone inside that cafe just now?" he asked Framp.

Framp looked. "No. No I don't."

"Neither do I. Nor any other human presence elsewhere." He looked all around, examining every visible window, every hidden point that might conceal a watching eye. "I think we have no witnesses just now."

"Witnesses to what?"

"To that birdlike flight I mentioned." He stepped closer to Framp, pushing him up against the landing's rail. "Terrible what liquor does to a man, how it makes it difficult for him to walk, sometimes even to stand. I've heard of drunks falling from high places while intoxicated, or while sickened the morning after. And you, sir, are a drunk. A hungover drunk."

Framp felt a burst of confusion and panic. What was this man talking about, and what was he about to—

Framp got his answer even before he could frame the question.

Ulysses shoved him, hard, tilting him out over the railing and then shoving again. "Take your flight, bird!" the Englishman said. Framp's feet left the landing and he pitched out into space, falling to the hard-packed alley below.

Ulysses heard the snap of the neck bone all the way up on the landing. Framp's body relaxed and spread limply, almost like the jelly Ulysses had spread across his biscuit at the breakfast table that morning.

Ulysses vanished back into the hotel, went past Framp's room and closed the door. He'd let someone else "discover" the body in the alley.

He had some searching to do—he had to find whoever now possessed that manuscript.

Laurel recognized the horse as soon as it came sauntering down the slope toward her. It had been the peddler's horse, the one pulling his wagon. She wasn't sure what would have drawn it back here from wherever Uncle Framp had abandoned it. She wondered if beasts were sometimes drawn back to the places their masters died. She'd never heard of such a thing, but something had made this horse find its way back here, even though this was not its home. One thing seemed certain to her: It was a sign, an indication that a prayer she'd been making the last hour had gotten its answer.

She'd awakened that morning with the distinct feeling that her father needed her, and that she should go after him and find him.

Especially with Uncle Framp out there somewhere. She was scared of her uncle now, for she knew him better ever since he'd killed that peddler. He'd proven by that act that he was indeed every bit as bad a fellow as her father had at times said he was . . . no, worse. She doubted that even Billy Sawyer would have thought Framp had it in him to kill a peddler with a knife just because . . . because what? She couldn't even recall the reason he'd given for the act, if he'd ever given one at all.

She'd felt that urge to go after her father, but it hadn't much mattered. She was stuck here, no way to travel. But she'd walked out to the barn, thinking things over, and had spotted there an old saddle, thrown over the wall of a bin. It was worn out, the leather cracked and ugly, but it was a saddle with all its parts, and she'd taken it as a sign from above. So she'd started her prayer: "God, if you'll send me a horse that this saddle will fit, I'll go ride after Papa. I know he was heading for Dodge, so if I do the same, I should be able to find him. Maybe I'll find him coming back, with that book of Mr. Farnsworth's delivered to him and his reward in his pocket. If that happens, I pray, Lord, that we'll be able soon to go to Chicago and get my operation done. Then I'll walk again, like girls are supposed to, and I'll even dance. I'll dance for you, God, to show you how grateful I am."

She'd prayed that prayer over and over again, not thinking a lot about it and neither expecting nor doubting an answer. She'd just prayed, saying the words in her mind, waiting for whatever would happen, or not happen. But when she'd seen the horse coming over the hill, she'd known her prayer had made it all the way to God's ear. And He'd seen fit to reply, sending her the horse she'd asked for.

It was hard for a young, crippled girl to deal with saddling a grown horse, but she managed after three tries to get the saddle placed. The bridle went into place, first try. Then she gave the horse some oats she found in the barn, packaged up some more for the road in a burlap bag, and tied the horse securely.

She went back into the house and began packing food for herself. She had no idea how long it would take her to ride to Dodge. Nor could she guess what weather she would encounter, or what strangers she'd run across. Being as young and physically impaired as she was, she knew that some might seek to "help" her in ways that proved troublesome or interfering. And then there were the kind of people her father had warned her about, those who were simply bad to the core and would take advantage of anyone they saw as weak.

It wouldn't take much for her to talk herself out of making the journey at all. But two thoughts kept her on course. One was the knowledge that her father was out there alone, and had not contacted her. On one prior occasion he'd left her in the care of family friends while he made a necessary journey, and twice while he was gone he'd wired back messages to her so she would know he was well. The telegrams had been delivered right to her door.

There was a telegraph office in Rockfield, too, and as far as Laurel knew, it had survived the tornado. Of course, there were probably wires down everywhere, and a telegraph office could hardly function without wires. That probably explained the lack of communication—but maybe not. Maybe something had happened to her father. Maybe he was hurt, or sick, or . . .

She would not let herself consider the other possibility.

The second thought that kept her aimed toward her journey was the one she'd already thought through: the fact that the horse had showed up just at the time she prayed for one. That had to mean something, didn't it? It had to mean that she was supposed to make the journey. And if she did what she was supposed to do, surely the same providence that had sent the horse to her would also take care of her along the way.

She readied herself as best she could, tried to think of all situations and scenarios she might have to deal with as a traveler, and then she mounted up, said her mental goodbye to the house of her Uncle Framp, and headed out the same direction her father had, bound for Dodge.

Billy Sawyer rode deep in thought, trying to figure out the scenario in which he found himself. He couldn't shake from his mind the notion that the thief who had robbed him in the grove and taken the manuscript was someone he knew. Though the face had been covered and the man had uttered no words, there was something so familiar in his movements, his posture, his attitudes, that Billy was simply certain.

And in an odd way, the man had shown Billy some mercy. He'd not killed him, for one thing, and had left his bonds loose enough that Billy had managed to free himself. It had taken a day and a half of effort, but he'd done it. And then he'd found his horse. The thief hadn't even stolen his horse.

Why? Why would a thief behave in such a manner? Did he not know he was opening himself to being followed once Billy got free?

And there was another twist: the theft of the manuscript itself. There was little inherent worth in a box of papers. That was not something that would be commonly stolen like jewels or cash. Whoever took the manuscript had known what he was taking. The manuscript's value lay strictly in the fact it was an unfinished Farnsworth. So the thief had to have known what Billy possessed, had to have known exactly what it was. The way he had carried out the robbery had been focused and precise. He'd come in not to take potluck with whatever some random traveler had, but specifically to recover the manuscript.

Billy rode along, pondering, and suddenly he reined his horse to a halt. He frowned at the landscape ahead of him, then turned and looked behind him, realizations clicking together in his head.

With a deflating, disturbing comprehension it all became clear. Billy rolled his head on his shoulders, trying to work out the residual soreness caused by his awkward posture against that tree, and said aloud, "Framp."

Of course it had been Framp! That was the person whose posture and mannerisms he'd recognized! Who else but Framp would have been positioned to figure out he had the manuscript? And Framp would have had reason not to harm Billy in a lasting way. It all fit. It all made sense.

But it raised a disturbing question. If it was Framp who had robbed him, that meant either that he had brought Laurel with him, and kept her out of sight while he robbed her father, or that Laurel was abandoned back at the house, alone.

Billy had to go back. He'd lost the manuscript now; the odds of tracking down Framp weren't good because Framp would be trying to evade him. And if he did find

Framp, what could he do? Steal back the manuscript? That wasn't the way Billy Sawyer worked, and Framp would certainly not be cooperative.

No, it was time to give up this entire fantasy of gaining wealth from a famous author. For Billy Sawyer there would be no reward from Farnsworth for the return of his lost volume. No immediate surgery for Laurel. And that was the part that really hurt. How would he tell his daughter that her dream had to be deferred? And for how long? It was beginning to feel as if he would never be able to give his girl the gift of strong legs and freedom from crutches.

It broke his heart to think of it.

He turned his horse and began slowly riding back the way he'd come. He had to find his daughter, had to know that she was safe and well.

Jack Domino had been sheriff of Berry County for only three years, but in that time the job had aged him a decade. Hair that was once black was now gray; hair that was once present was now gone. But he stuck the job out, and would until the end, because it was his duty, and because the people of his county for the most part made it all worthwhile.

And one thing was certain: In the business of sheriffing, one could never guess what a new day would bring. Domino had awakened this particular morning expecting nothing but a routine kind of day, probably no real happenings . . . and now, here he was looking across his desk at a young man who was telling him he'd witnessed a murder over in the nearby town of Fairwater. A man pushing another off the landing of the exterior staircase at the Fairwater Hotel. Right in broad daylight! It seemed an unlikely story to Domino, but one thing kept him from discounting it: He knew the family of young Jim Barker, knew his father especially, and knew the young man to be a levelheaded kind of fellow just like his sire. And the cafe the family operated was just across the street from the hotel in Fairwater, so it was believable that Jim could easily have witnessed such an act, if it occurred.

"Sheriff, I get the strongest feeling you don't believe me," Jim said. He'd ridden over to the sheriff's office on the family's wagon, and was pretty thoroughly talked out. He hoped he wouldn't have to weave some elaborate defense of his claims.

"Jim, I put great confidence in anything I hear from the Barker family. It's just an odd thing to hear, you know. What would compel a man to commit such a public murder? If he wanted to kill the other man, it seems he would have done it back inside the hotel, or some other hidden place, so as not to risk being seen."

"I've thought about that myself, Sheriff," Jim said. "As best I can figure it, he didn't think there was anyone there to see him. It was just past breakfast, and the customers—including the murderer—had cleared out of the place. From where he was up on that landing, all he could have seen were the tables just inside the front window. And they were empty. He'd been sitting at one of them himself, with a woman."

"And where did the woman go?"

"She'd already left the hotel and gone down the street, very upset and emotional. I got the strong notion she was in love with this Ulysses Church fellow, if that's really who he is, but that he didn't have much of the same kind of feeling back toward her. Although she talked about how he'd killed a man because of her, which she took as proof that he loved her."

"Killed a man? Any details on that?"

"No, sir. She declared that this Church fellow had killed a man because of her, but he said he killed the fellow because he'd insulted and threatened him, not because of her."

"Interesting. Quite interesting. One of the Ames boys was killed in a shooting out on the plains . . . have you heard that?"

"The ranching Ames boys?"

"That's right. Apparently shot by some man who approached a kind of party going on out by the woods up north of your town. There were some soiled doves there, which can give you a notion of what kind of party this was. And the one of them that has talked to my deputy says the man had a British way of speaking."

"Maybe it was Ulysses Church. Or whoever."

"You seem to doubt that this Church fellow is who he claims to be. Why?"

"I have this feeling that maybe he's somebody different. Somebody who is hiding behind a different name because he's trying to protect his reputation."

"Who?"

"I'm thinking maybe he's Charles Farnsworth."

"No! Why do you think that?"

"Because he's British, and in this part of the country. And because the woman with him said something about him looking for a manuscript. You know about the book Farnsworth lost his pages for, I guess."

"Indeed. I've heard the story. It's even made the papers."

"Well, there was a man in a saloon over in Fairwater

last night who was saying he had found the manuscript and was going to sell it back to Farnsworth. That was what made this English fellow so interested in him. When we saw a stranger coming out of the hotel, down the stairs, he decided it must be the same man who'd been saying he had the lost book, and that's what made him leave the cafe to go find him."

"Interesting." The sheriff leaned back in his chair and steepled his fingers, thinking. "So perhaps we have a world-famous writer visiting Kansas who just might also be a murderer. But why would he have killed that man over that manuscript?"

"Well, maybe he didn't like it that the fellow wanted money to give it back to him. Maybe he didn't figure he owed him."

"I don't know . . . the papers have it that Farnsworth has already publicly offered a reward to get the book back."

"I don't pretend to know the answers, Sheriff. All I'm telling you is what I saw, and I saw a man pushed off a hotel landing. By the way, Ulysses Church denied to me that he is Farnsworth. But he also said that Farnsworth isn't Farnsworth, which makes no sense to me."

"Maybe it was his way of saying Farnsworth is some kind of fraud or fake."

"Maybe. He did talk about Farnsworth like he knew him, and said he was a better man than Farnsworth is."

"In all my years as sheriff, this is the oddest situation I've run across, Jim. One more question for you: Why didn't you tell all this to my deputy over in Fairwater? Why'd you come this far just to find me?"

"My father always told me to talk to the highest authorities when it's about something important. And he says you are a good man, and to be trusted. And besides that, I had an errand here in White Fork anyway."

Domino nodded. "Well, Jim, thank you for your visit. You'll be heading back home now?"

"Yes, sir. I was hoping you might ride back with me."

"I will. I need to ask quite a few questions around Fairwater, it seems."

"Is there time for me to pick up a few things? There's a new bunch of dishes my mother has bought for the cafe, and they're in at the freight office. That's the errand I was talking about."

"I'll go with you. You brought your wagon, I'm assuming."

"I did."

"Come on, son. Let's go fetch those dishes, then go take a new look at this murder you witnessed."

When the sheriff came walking out of his office accompanied by a young man, Lonzo Wallace stepped back into the shadows of an alley across and slightly down the street from the Berry County Sheriff's Office. In his hand was a metal box containing papers, manuscript papers. He'd taken the box from the room of that poor old drunken fellow he'd helped across the street the night before over in Fairwater, where he'd started the evening by drinking and complaining about his lot in life, and the difficulties of finding a way to make any decent money. Then he'd ended up talking to that drunk fellow whose lips had been too loose for his own good. The fool never should have bragged about having the lost Farnsworth manuscript that everyone in the region was so aware of. Information like that a man should keep to himself. Talking too much can cost a man, and it had cost that fellow when Lonzo spirited the manuscript out of his room.

But once he had it in hand, Lonzo had been unsure what to do with it. He and everyone else for miles around knew that Farnsworth was offering a reward for the return of his pages, but Lonzo wasn't sure how to go about finding the man. And he wondered, too, how he could know he had the authentic manuscript. It certainly seemed unlikely there would be two metal boxes with manuscript pages in them . . . but for Lonzo Wallace things involving writing, words, and such were not things about which he could be sure of himself. He could read his name and a few words such as "the" and "dog" and "boy," but beyond that he was illiterate.

For all he knew, the box he had might contain someone's old love letters. He simply couldn't be sure, on his own.

But there was someone here in the county seat who could help him, a man who had been kind to him in times past and who knew much about the world of books. And well he should, for he sold them for a living. The Stewart Book Shop stood on Main Street, just down from where Lonzo was, and Jake Stewart, proprietor, was a trustworthy man who Lonzo could turn to without fear of betrayal. He would be able to look at the manuscript and tell quickly if it was authentic. And unlike others, he wouldn't try to steal it away.

Lonzo had brought along one of the two extra shirts he owned, so he could hide the metal manuscript box. He wrapped the shirt around it and tucked the package under his arm. It wouldn't do for people to see the metal box. The newspapers, he had been told by more literate friends, had been carrying descriptions of Farnsworth's lost item, and folks might figure things out if they saw him carrying a metal box into a bookshop.

Lonzo whistled and tried to look nonchalant as he walked down the street and up onto the boardwalk leading to the bookshop. Lord, this business of carrying a stolen item made him nervous! He'd been nervous even before coming into town, and to see the sheriff walking out the door of his office had made him even more so. But the sheriff hadn't lingered. He'd gotten onto his horse and ridden off alongside a wagon driven by a younger fellow, a fellow who looked familiar to Lonzo. Oh, yes. He remembered. That boy was the one who worked in the Hot Skillet Cafe back in Fairwater. Lonzo wondered what had brought him here.

He reached the bookshop and glanced through the window. Good! There was old Mr. Stewart behind the sales counter, examining an old volume through his thick spectacles. Lonzo went to the door, opened it, and entered.

Chapter Fourteen

"Well! Lonzo, isn't it?" Stewart asked, looking over the wire rims of his glasses. "What brings you to town today? Cattle business not keeping you busy enough?"

"Truth is, sir, I got something I need you to look at. Something you mustn't tell nobody about. You got to promise me that . . . please?"

"Sounds serious, Lonzo."

"I don't know . . . maybe it is. Can I trust you?"

"Of course you can. What do you have? An old book?"

"No sir. A new one. One that ain't even really a book yet." Lonzo pulled back the shirt covering the manuscript box and showed it nervously to Stewart.

Stewart eyed the gleaming brazen box, looking confused at first. But comprehension began to dawn, and it showed in his eyes.

"How did you come by *that*, of all things . . . if it is what I suspect it is?"

"I'd as soon not say. Let's just say a feller over at Fairwater had it, and he'd found it stuck up in a tree over near Rockfield where the storm was. And he passed it on to me."

"Willingly?"

"Well, he didn't say or do nothing to stop me."

"I'll ask no further questions along those lines. Not sure I really want to hear the answers," Stewart said. "Now, what do you want me to tell you about your treasure there?"

"I need to know if it really is a treasure or not. I need to know if it's really something wrote by that famous writer fellow."

"I'll take a look. I'm familiar enough with his style that I think I can tell by the flow of his words. And I suspect it is authentic even before I look. How many metal boxes containing manuscripts can there be bouncing around this particular part of Kansas, after all?"

"My thinking too, Mr. Stewart. Here . . . take a look . . . but if somebody comes in, do you mind covering it up?"

"Rest assured, I will. In the meantime, for further insurance, would you lock that door behind you? And turn over the little sign hanging there. We'll just close up shop a few minutes."

Lonzo locked the door and turned the sign. Through the door's window glass he noticed that the sky to the northeast was beginning to look dark and strange. And the wind was up.

"May be another round of bad weather coming in up toward Rockfield," he said to Stewart.

"Yes . . . I noticed the clouds. Not what those poor folks need," Stewart said. "They've had enough bad weather already."

"Ain't that the truth!"

Stewart opened the metal box and began looking at the papers. "Well, the name on the top of the pages is correct, in any case: *Mortimer Straw*."

"So it's really his book?"

"Hold on . . . let me look more closely."

Stewart squinted through his glasses and began reading. His lips moved silently as he read, his eyes shifting back and forth across the lines.

"Does it sound like Farnsworth's writing?" asked Lonzo.

"Indeed it does . . . but there's something here I need to take a closer look at." True to his statement, he pulled the page up closer and read even more intently. Then he dug the full stack of pages out of the box and flipped through them quickly, pausing a little less than halfway through and looking puzzled.

"What is it?" Lonzo asked.

Stewart looked up at him. "Lonzo, might I ask your permission to hold this book a day or so? There are some questions I have about it that will take time to answer."

"Well . . . I guess a day or two won't hurt nothing. I been broke for years, so what's another couple of days?"

"Indeed." Stewart smiled, causing his white mustache to spread and rise. "I'll guard this carefully and keep it hidden from public view."

"All righty."

"Are you sure you don't mind me holding it for you?"

"Not at all. I figure it's probably safer here than in my

old butterfingers. I'd probably drop the thing out of a saddlebag or some such."

"Bosh! I'm sure it will be in good hands once it's back in yours. Thank you for sharing this with me, Lonzo. It is quite interesting indeed. Quite interesting." He paused and looked more serious. "But I should tell you that I do have a doubt about it. It indeed appears to be the authentic work of Charles Oliver Farnsworth . . . yet the words strike me as too familiar. And I've run across the name of a character in this story, one who died in the novel *The Carfax Years*, one of Farnsworth's earlier works."

"Well . . . maybe he has this story taking place in the time before that person kicked off. Reckon?"

"Possibly. But there is such a familiarity about these words . . . it's as if someone has taken an older Farnsworth work and recopied it, putting a new title, *Mortimer Straw*, at the top."

"Good Lord! Why would they do that?"

"I haven't the foggiest notion."

"Damn! There goes my reward. Farnsworth ain't going to pay to get back a copy of a book he had published years and years ago."

"I doubt he would. But I'm sure he'd be intrigued by the mystery of why this copying was done. As am I."

"I'll check back with you in a couple of days, Mr. Stewart. Thank you for your help. If I do end up with a reward somehow, I'll give you a part of it."

"Very kind of you, Lonzo. But you needn't feel obliged."

Lonzo smiled, nodded, and went on his way.

* * *

As Lonzo left, he unlocked the door and flipped the sign on it back to its OPEN side. But when he was gone, Stewart reclosed the place and locked the door again.

He went back to the counter, pulled up the high stool he often sat on, and made himself comfortable with the manuscript before him. He looked at it, frowning, flipping pages, comparing them, becoming so engrossed that when his big black tomcat named Cephas leaped up to the countertop and walked toward his master, Stewart almost fell off his stool in surprise. He looked over at the cat, laughed at himself, and scratched Cephas behind the right ear.

"Cephas, friend, I hate to lie to such a simple soul as Lonzo, but I had no choice. Oh, I didn't lie to him totally . . . there is certainly something odd about this manuscript . . . but I did lie to him about what it was. This is no copy of an earlier Farnsworth book. But look at this, cat. Look!" He held up papers as if the cat could actually read them. "Here are the opening pages of Chapter Six. Note the handwriting, Cephas. Can you see that? Now . . . here, deeper in the stack, more pages . . . exactly the same as these! A word-for-word copy. Same chapter, same words. But one difference: A different hand wrote this one. Clearly one is a copy of the other. It appears that Farnsworth, or someone, at least, is in the process of copying an existing manuscript, putting it into his own handwriting. But the copying isn't yet complete. Only some of the chapters, the first half or so of the manuscript, have been copied. Remarkable!"

He laid the papers down, picked up the cat, and sat it in his lap. He stroked its head and back, and Cephas settled in comfortably and began to purr.

"Do you know what I think is happening here, Cephas? I think we're seeing a case of plagiarism in progress. I think Farnsworth is making a copy of an existing manuscript, and disguising it as his own work by putting it in his own handwriting." He shook his head. "Remarkable! Earth-shaking in the world of popular literature, actually. For if Farnsworth is copying a manuscript for his newest book, might he have copied manuscripts for some, even all, of his earlier ones? And if so, who wrote them? Who is the *real* Charles Oliver Farnsworth, Cephas? Hmmm? Who is the true creative mind behind his work?"

He scratched Cephas some more, then laughed at himself. "Cephas, am I a fool? Am I drawing too many conclusions, extreme conclusions, based on no more than these two stacks of paper? Perhaps so. Farnsworth a plagiarist? It seems unlikely, on its face. But who can be sure? And if my explanation is not valid, what explanation is? If Farnsworth wrote the original work, then why is it in a handwriting different from the copy currently in progress? And if he is not plagiarizing the original, why is he bothering to recopy an entire manuscript when the first copy seems to be complete and well done? It can only be for purposes of disguising its true origin."

He rolled his head back, closing eyes to relieve strain. "Ah, Cephas! Who would have thought such a thing would come to light in such a humble place as our little shop? Hmmm? Who would have thought it? And what are we to do with this information? Hmmm? Right now, you see, you and I are the only ones who know about this. Other than Farnsworth himself, and perhaps the true author of that manuscript over there."

* * *

Sheriff Domino looked down on the dead face of Framp Rupert, a man whose name and origins he did not know. Jim Barker had never been in the back room of the local funeral parlor before, and was quite ill at ease, unable to look for long at the corpse. Every time he did, he relived the moment from that morning when he'd seen the Englishman shove this fellow over the railing to the ground a story below.

Jim headed for the door, wanting some fresh air. He passed through the outer parlor and out to the board-walk. A man passed and Jim looked up at him. "Mr. Banks!" he called. "Mr. Banks! Can I talk to you a minute?"

Banks, just one more of scores of local cowboys, turned. "Hello, Jimbo! You still serving up them good biscuits at the cafe?"

"I surely am. Come in tomorrow and I'll slip you a few to take back to the bunkhouse with you."

"You got a deal there, friend."

"Mr. Banks . . ."

"Call me Harve. I feel old enough already without the 'mister.'"

"All right, Harve. I need to ask you something."

"Shoot."

"Were you in the saloon last night?"

"You going to scold me if I was?"

"No, no. I leave the scolding to my father. He's the deacon, not me. But I do wonder if you happened to be there because there was a fellow in the saloon last night, I'm told, who said he had that missing manuscript of that Farnsworth fellow. You heard about that?"

"I've heard talk. Didn't pay it much heed because I

don't care a fig for books. But in fact, there was a man in there talking about that. He and Lonzo Wallace got into some kind of argument . . . Lonzo had been whining about not being able to make any money and get ahead in life, and this fellow proceeded to tell him the way he was going to get ahead was to sell Farnsworth's missing book back to him. Said he already had it."

"Would you know this man if you saw him again?"

"Probably so."

"Step inside, Harve."

Harve Banks nodded. "That's him, Sheriff. That's the man who was talking in the saloon last night about having that missing book."

"You're sure of it?"

"I am. He and Lonzo Wallace had an exchange or two, and Lonzo ended up walking him back across the street to his hotel room. This fellow here was so drunk he could hardly walk at all."

"They tell me that this manuscript was not in this man's room at the hotel when they looked through it after he was found dead."

"I don't know nothing about that, sir. All I know is that he claimed he had it."

"Might this Lonzo have taken it after he walked this fellow to the hotel?"

"Well, anything's possible. Lonzo will pull the odd little trick every now and again, if he thinks he can make some money with it. Not trying to talk bad about him, because he's a good fellow at heart. But a fact is a fact. But I'll tell you one thing for a fact, Sheriff: Lonzo would never kill nobody, not for no reason, money or whatever. So if you think he done that, I know you're wrong."

"We know who killed this man. Jim there witnessed the murder. It was an English fellow who called himself Ulysses Church. But Jim has a notion that might not be his real name."

"Who is he, then?"

"Maybe Farnsworth himself. He's British like Farnsworth is, so maybe he *is* Farnsworth."

"I thought Farnsworth was pretty well known. Folks would recognize the real one, wouldn't they?"

"If they've seen him, they would. I've never laid eyes on the man, nor has Jim and most other folks. He was up in Rockfield when they had the big storm, but most folks here weren't."

"Speaking of storms, it looks to be building up to one again, up to the northeast."

"I noticed. Lord have mercy, this weather!"

Harve looked down at Framp's corpse again, thinking things through. "So it may be that this man got hold of Farnsworth's missing book, and Farnsworth found out about it, went up, got his book, and shoved this one over the rail just to make a point."

"It could be. But we don't know it was Farnsworth. Nor whether the manuscript disappeared at the same time this man was killed, or sometime before. If it was left unguarded in that room, it could have been took by any number of folks."

"Sounds like this Ulysses, or Farnsworth, or who-ever he really is, is somebody worth finding, Sheriff," Harve said.

"So he is. And we'll find him. We will. And we'll get

to the bottom of this thing just like this dead one here got to the bottom of that alley by the hotel this morning." The sheriff threw back his head and laughed at his own highly inappropriate joke. Harve laughed, too. Jim didn't have it in him even to smile.

Chapter Fifteen

Billy Sawyer was a worried man. The farther he rode back in the direction of Framp's house, where he hoped and prayed Laurel was still safe, the more threatening the weather became. The sky was cloudy but oddly lighted, and the wind was strong and growing stronger every passing minute. All in all, the weather was like it had been before the storm that wiped out so much of Rockfield. Billy was all but sure that more of the same was on its way, and it made him feel sick to his soul, and all the more worried about Laurel.

He cursed the name of Framp Rupert for having deserted her. He'd given the man too much credit, thinking that he cared enough about Laurel to do the right thing for her sake. Clearly he did not. He'd abandoned her, headed out after Billy, and robbed him of the manuscript, not even being enough of a man to show his face when he did it.

And now Laurel was left alone, most likely, back there in that little house. And this time the storm might not spare the house as it had the first time. Laurel could be caught helpless. Billy prayed she would have enough wit about her to find the right kind of shelter, even if she had to go crawl into one of the caves in the hill behind Framp's house.

Billy knew he would not make it back before the weather turned its worst. As much as he'd like to be where Laurel was if a tornado did strike, the sensible thing for him to do was to find shelter of his own, within reach.

The road upon which Billy traveled wound around a stand of trees. As he made that turn, Billy was met with the sight of a man, probably in his sixties, standing at the open front gate of a fenced-in yard surrounding a beautiful, two-story house. When he saw Billy, the man waved his hands above his head, signaling for him to stop.

"Good day, sir," Billy said as he rode up and halted. "I think we're about to have some weather."

"Oh, yes, sir. A cyclone has already been seen. Saw it myself, in fact, over that way. Not as big, I think, as the one that damaged Rockfield, but a frightening sight nevertheless. And we could see much worse ones form in these weather conditions. God bless us! There's no telling how bad it could become."

"I've been thinking just the same, Mr. . . . ."

"Carlyle. Andrew Carlyle. And I'm not a 'mister,' but a reverend."

"I've heard of you, sir. You preach at the Presbyterian church house over near Fairwater."

"That's me, sir. And you are . . ."

"Billy Sawyer. I clerked in the mercantile over at Rockfield until that cyclone flipped it off the map like a finger flipping a bug off a table."

"Colorful way with words, you have. Please, Mr. Sawyer, come in and take shelter with us. We have a large cellar, quite safe, and we've already got guests here, Mrs. Carlyle and I, because our cellar is the safest place we can be." He paused. "Sawyer. You did say your name was Sawyer?"

"Yes, sir. You got it right."

"Interesting. One of our guests already here is also named Sawyer. A beautiful, sweet young lady with blond hair. Crippled a bit, sadly. But a wonderful child."

Billy came down off the saddle. "Laurel is *here?*"

"She is. She rode by maybe an hour ago, the wind all but pushing her off her saddle. I felt quite sorry for her. She said she was heading for Dodge, looking for her father."

"Reverend Carlyle, I *am* her father. Is she all right?"

"Why, yes . . . as all right as a young crippled girl can be who has been left to her own devices and abandoned to have to seek out her loved ones entirely on her own." He paused. "Sir, I'm sorry. I speak too harshly, not knowing the circumstances of why she was left alone."

"You speak no more harshly than I've spoken to myself lately," Billy replied. "But I didn't leave her alone. I left her in the care of her uncle. He abandoned her in order to go out and do something he shouldn't have done. He did not have my permission to do so, nor was I aware of it." He hesitated, frowning. "Did you say she was riding on a horse?"

"Yes, sir. That one there, looking at us out of the barn stall."

"I don't recognize that horse. I wonder where she got it."

"Come in and ask her. I'm sure she'll be thrilled to see her father."

"I know I'll be happy to see her. I've been worried about her ever since I found out her uncle left her. I was on my way home when this weather moved in."

"Come inside, sir. I'll bring young Laurel up from the cellar so you can meet her in privacy in the parlor. There's a goodly little crowd in the cellar, and you may want a few moments to talk with her without an audience."

"You're a fine man, Reverend. I thank you and accept your offer of shelter."

"Put your horse in the barn, then. I'll lend a hand. Then we'll go in."

Billy stood in the parlor, looking at a painting of George Washington on the wall, waiting in odd nervousness for the reverend to bring Laurel up to meet him. He was grateful that she was all right, but concerned that she'd been out riding across the countryside alone, with no protector at all other than whatever guardian angels the Almighty provided to young crippled girls.

He heard them then, the reverend's footsteps coming up the stairs from the cellar, and lighter footsteps, too, mixed in with the familiar tapping of Laurel's crutches. His heart raced; his eagerness to see her threatened to overwhelm his emotions.

Indeed he could not withhold his tears when she appeared in the doorway, looking at him with an expression of love and, for some reason, relief. "Papa!" she said, and came toward him, as adept and swift as ever on her crutches. The reverend watched, smiling, then stepped aside to give them the privacy he'd promised.

He swept her into his arms and all but crushed her with a hug. When he let go she had to gasp for air a minute or so, for he had squeezed her so hard she'd been unable to breathe.

"Laurel, thank God you're all right. I'm sorry I ever left you with Framp. I know he deserted you. He shouldn't have . . . but more than that, I shouldn't have ever left you to start with."

"Papa, I have to tell you something about Uncle Framp. He did a bad, bad thing, Papa."

Billy figured she couldn't know the half of it. Framp had robbed his own brother-in-law, and left him tied to a tree to fend for himself and find his freedom by all but tearing the hide from his wrists and hands. But what Laurel said next made Billy's story seem trivial by comparison.

"Uncle Framp killed a man, Papa. A peddler who came by, somebody he'd known before and had trouble with. Uncle Framp said it was an accident, but I saw it and I could tell he did it on purpose. He fell and stuck a knife in the man. Then he carried off his body and hid it so nobody would know."

"Framp killed someone, with you watching?"

"He did." She began to cry. "That's where I got the horse to come looking for you. It was the peddler's horse. It's a good old horse, but it's tired and it's old, and I think it's a sad horse. I think it knows its master is dead."

Billy hugged his daughter gently, trying to comfort her. "Honey, Framp proved to be a worse fellow than I ever knew or thought. He robbed me, dear. Put on a mask and stuck me up at gunpoint and tied me to a tree, never saying a word. He hoped I wouldn't know him, but after he was gone I figured out it was him. He left me tied, to fend for myself. See my wrists? That's where the ropes were."

"He took your money?"

"No, honey. He took the manuscript."

She looked up at Billy. "Then he took *my* money . . . the money that would make me able to walk."

"I guess so, Laurel. But we must try to forgive him. That's our duty, to be forgiving."

Her emotions were on edge, though, and all she could do at that point was cry and say, through trembling lips, "I think I hate him, Papa."

"It's hard not to, Laurel. I understand. But try not to, if you can."

"Listen to the wind, Papa. It sounds like it did before the big storm back at home."

She was right. He listened to the howl and roar of the rising storm, and realized he needed to get his daughter back to the cellar. "Come on, Laurel. Show me the place the reverend is letting people take shelter."

"He's a nice man, Papa. And his wife is, too. And the other people down there have been kind to me, too. There's only one person who hasn't said anything to me."

"People pulled together in dangerous situations often are good to one another that way," Billy said.

The cellar was large, almost the size of the house in length and breadth. Though much of it was taken up by well-laden shelves with vegetables and such in jars, about half of it was lined with rough lumber and finished off into a rugged but sturdy room, lit by kerosene lamps attached to the walls. In that area was a little con-glomeration of people, seated on random stray chairs, crates, casks, and the like. When Billy came down with Laurel, they stood and welcomed him warmly, most of them saying what a fine girl Laurel was. Billy shook hands all around, Laurel making introductions. He was impressed that his daughter was so able to remember names.

Only one member of the party had not joined in the almost festive mood of welcome. He sat in a corner on an old, battered chair, leaning forward and staring at the hard-packed dirt floor between his feet. Laurel tugged Billy's sleeve. "That's the man I ain't met yet, Papa," she said.

Billy walked over to him. "Hello, sir," he said. "Since we're to ride out a storm together, we may as well know one another. My name is Billy Sawyer. This is my daughter, Laurel." He stuck out his hand.

The man looked up and stood slowly. Billy backed away, astonished.

"Good to see you again, Mr. Sawyer," said Charles Oliver Farnsworth, grabbing Billy's hand and shaking it. Billy noticed Farnsworth's hand felt cold and clammy, and that his brow was sweating more than the dirt walls on the unfinished side of the cellar. "I hope you'll pardon my lack of vigor. I seem to be taking ill with some malady or another." Then Farnsworth yanked his hand out of Billy's and put it to his mouth to cover a cough.

"Good to see you again, sir. I've been looking for you lately," Billy said, pondering inwardly the odd turns of life.

"Looking for me? Why?"

"I had something that belongs to you. Something that the last storm took away from you."

Farnsworth's mouth dropped open. "My manuscript?"

"Yes, sir. But it was taken away from me by another man, a fellow named Framp Rupert. I had planned to give it back to you, but he plans to hold it for ransom, so to speak. To try to make you pay higher than whatever reward you had in mind."

"Where is this Rupert fellow now?"

"Probably somewhere around Dodge, looking for you. That was the last place anyone knew you to be going. I was headed for Dodge myself when he robbed me."

"I didn't linger long at Dodge. My reception there was not as warm as that I received in your unfortunate little town. And I came back this way in hope that, by making myself easier to find in the vicinity in which I lost the manuscript, the manuscript might more readily come back to me."

"A sensible thought."

"I had a further intention as well. I was impressed by the library in Rockfield, and sorry at its destruction. It had crossed my mind to perhaps arrange a donation to the librarian to start a rebuilding project."

Good. Farnsworth was an altruistic man. That would make him more likely to help out Laurel.

"But now, I am at a loss. How can I find this Rupert?"

"I don't know. He lives near Rockfield, within sight of it, actually, though across the county line. He may return there . . . or he may not. My daughter tells me he was involved in the killing of a peddler. That might cause him to seek a new place to be. I honestly don't know what he'll do. I thought I knew the man . . . it winds up I really didn't. Even though I married his sister."

"No! Really? Where is your wife? Not with you and your lovely daughter today?"

"She's passed away, sir. Some years ago now."

"I'm quite sorry. But you have a lovely angel here to keep you company." He leaned forward to shake hands with Laurel, as friendly now as he had been aloof before. "Pleased to meet you, Miss. My name is Mr. Farnsworth."

She shook his hand, beaming up at him. He smiled back. Billy wondered what she was thinking. Probably that she was shaking hands with the man who would make it possible for her to walk normally.

But now that the manuscript was gone, the prospect of obtaining aid from Farnsworth seemed unlikely. Damn Framp Rupert! The man's theft had robbed not only Billy, but Laurel most of all.

Farnsworth, clearly not feeling well, sat down again. Laurel found a wooden box in the cellar and brought it over to sit beside him. She and the writer talked quietly, Billy watching from a few yards away. It seemed to him Laurel and Farnsworth were getting on especially well. And though he hated to think in so mercenary a way, he realized that that couldn't hurt. If Farnsworth grew fond of Laurel, he would be more willing to lend a hand toward her medical needs, if ever the situation came around to that.

Chapter Sixteen

The storm progressed as expected in some ways, becoming tornadic, but after that all predictability vanished. The twister, unseen by any in the reverend's home because they were all huddled praying in the cellar, lifted high and rode the crest of the sky for miles before at last descending near the Berry County courthouse, just up the street from the bookshop where old Mr. Stewart huddled with his cat and his new treasure, the mysterious Farnsworth double manuscript. He was clutching hard to both cat and manuscript box when the twister fingered down from the clouds and tore his bookshop off the map, sending lumber, glass, shelves and books flying in all directions. As had been the case in Rockfield when the library was destroyed, many of the flying books blew open and flapped through the sky like strange birds.

Stewart's flight was less graceful. He was picked up bodily, turned upside down, and carried for many yards through the sky before being slammed down hard on the roof of the Methodist Church. A local drunk saw his body roll down the sloping roof, pitch off, and fall to the ground, where he did not move again. He had lost the cat along the way—it was later found safe and uninjured—but he still clung to the manuscript box, which the drunk, who did not read newspapers, failed to know for what it was.

The drunk examined Stewart, but in his condition could not tell if he was living or dead. Panicking for a moment, he paced back and forth by the body, glaring down at it as if offended that Stewart had presented him such a dilemma. Then inspiration: He'd go seek the local doctor. He'd met the sawbones only once before, back when he'd fallen three months earlier and cracked a bone in his hand. But he liked the doctor, a young man whose father was a preacher named Carlyle.

Struggling against the horrific wind, he set off at a staggering lope in the direction of Carlyle's office, which was also the physician's home. He lived in rooms above the office area. When he got there he caught a glimpse, above the half-curtains, of Carlyle working in the examination room. He had an intent expression and beads of sweat on his brow.

The drunk entered the outer office, which was untended, and went straight to the examination-room door. He opened it without knocking and walked inside.

Dr. Carlyle turned in surprise and glared at him. "You can't just walk in here!" he said. "I'm treating a man with a gunshot wound."

"Well, there's another man needs treating, too."

"I'll get to you as quickly as I can. You look sound enough to me."

"Ain't me. It's a fellow who got pulled up in the air by the wind and slammed against the roof of the church-house. Then he rolled down and *kerplunk*. There he lay. I don't think he's dead yet."

"I'll go to him as fast as I can. I can't leave this man at this stage, or I'll lose him."

"Who is he?"

"I don't have time to talk."

The drunk got angry, face reddening. He slammed the heel of his fist down on a nearby tabletop, making glassware and various probes and pincers dance across the wood. "Damn it! I'll not be talked down to. I don't stand for folks talking down to me. Not even big fancy doctors."

Seeing the better part of discretion, Dr. Carlyle changed his manner dramatically, becoming friendly and respectful, hard as that was to do in such circumstances. "This man is a visiting Englishman, whose name, if I understood it, is Ulysses Church."

"Who shot him?"

"A woman. A woman of poor repute. A soiled dove."

"A whore?"

"Not to put too fine a point on it, yes. A whore. Someone he called Chastity. Odd name for such a kind of female."

"Why?"

"Because the word 'chastity' hardly associates with the kind of life a prostitute leads."

"No, I mean, why did she shoot him?"

"I don't know. People of that sort require little reason to do violence, I've found."

"Will he live?"

"He has a chance. If he will rest and let himself heal. If he abuses himself and worsens his wound, I cannot predict what will happen to him."

The drunk lingered, watching. The storm continued to howl outside. A mile away, the twister rose again and rode the sky, then descended to wipe out a barn and a grove of trees along a creekbank.

To the northwest, the house of the kindly Reverend Andrew Carlyle, father of the busy physician and host of the Sawyers, Farnsworth, and the other storm refugees, remained undamaged, buffeted now only by residual winds and large, pounding raindrops that blew horizontally against its walls.

Safe as they were, there was distress among those huddled in the reverend's cellar. Charles Farnsworth was ill, and growing more ill as time went by. He'd gone from pleasant conversation with Laurel to a nearly stupor-like state. His face was red and damp, his eyes half closed. By the time the storm was sufficiently past that the refugees became restless and eager to go back up and out, Farnsworth was sick at his stomach. He was able to stand with help, and to shuffle his feet enough to move with the aid of others, but by the time they reached the sodden outdoors and saw the storm clouds moving away toward the southwest, Farnsworth grew nauseated and vomited.

Laurel saw it happen and turned away, saying "Ooooooh," and weeping.

"Papa, is he going to die?" she asked Billy.

"No, honey, no. He's just gotten sick, that's all. He needs a doctor, though."

"We will take him to my son, who has a practice in operation over at the county seat," Rev. Carlyle said. "I know there is a doctor at Rockfield as well, but my son, I believe, is the superior physician. And the road is better to where he is than is the road to Rockfield."

"I think we should get him to your son as quickly as we can, then. Do you have a buggy or wagon?"

"I have a buggy, which my wife and I take to Sunday services each week. I'll drive him there in my buggy."

Billy saddled up his horse while the minister readied his buggy. They traveled together, Billy riding beside the buggy, Laurel riding behind him on the peddler's horse that now was hers. Farnsworth slumped in the seat beside Rev. Carlyle and was sick twice more before they finally reached their destination.

By the time they got there, Dr. Carlyle had left Ulysses Church alone, no longer on the operating table in the examination room, but in one of the beds in the hospital section of the practice, set up in a rear room. His presence was unknown to Billy Sawyer and Rev. Carlyle as they helped the watery-weak Farnsworth into the examination room, where they laid him down on the table where Church had been only minutes before.

"I will see if my son is upstairs," the Rev. Carlyle said, heading for the stairs. He was back again a minute later, shaking his head. "He must have been called out to someone injured in the storm."

To their surprise, Farnsworth spoke. "A pillow," he croaked out.

"Laurel," said Billy, "would you look around and see

if you can find a pillow for us to put under Mr. Farnsworth's head."

Laurel set off to her task. Finding nothing in the front, she headed into the back area, and came out fast, going to her father. "Papa, there's a man back there, in a bed. He has a bandage on him, and there's some blood."

"Did he frighten you?"

"Yes. He sat up. And he said, 'Who are you, girl?' He had a mean voice. And he talks like Mr. Farnsworth. Like he's from England."

Something clicked in Billy's mind, a possibility he didn't like to think about. "Stay in here, Laurel," he said. "I'll go check."

But by the time he got to the door, his dread suspicion had been confirmed. Ulysses Church walked in, bloodied and pale and looking like he belonged in a bed or maybe a grave. He eyed Billy, then the Rev. Carlyle, and finally his eye came to rest on Charles Farnsworth, who had drifted into slumber.

"Damn!" Ulysses said loudly. "How did *that* pile of manure end up here?"

"What's happened to you?" Billy asked.

"I was shot by a whore."

"My daughter is present, sir. Please watch your tongue."

"Hell with your daughter, and hell with you. And you, over there—you look like a parson. Are you?"

"I am a minister in the Methodist tradition."

"Hell with you, too. You ought to be happy there—I always picture hell as full of preachers and priests."

Farnsworth blubbered and opened his eyes, staring at the ceiling.

"Well," said Ulysses. "I think the bastard hears the voice of his superior."

Farnsworth slowly turned his head and focused on Ulysses, who grinned back at him evilly. Farnsworth surprised Billy by lifting himself up and swinging his legs down so that he was seated on the side of the examination table. His face was remarkably pallid and he stared at Ulysses without blinking.

"You must . . . keep him away . . . from me . . ." Farnsworth said to Billy. "Dangerous man . . ."

"Not as dangerous as I might be if I hadn't taken a bullet," Church said. "But dangerous enough." He looked at Billy and the Rev. Carlyle. "Gentlemen, you should know that I've been looking for our good Mr. Farnsworth for quite some time. I've followed him many a mile, over English brook and glen, over broad ocean waves and currents, and across hundreds upon hundreds of American miles. I knew that eventually I would find the end of my search. I confess I did not expect it to be today, or here."

"Beware of him," Farnsworth said. "He is a madman."

"He doesn't lie," Church said. "I've been mad for years. Driven mad by the robbery of what is rightfully mine, and by seeing wealth and fame go to a man who cannot write a coherent sentence, but who can most eloquently make claim to mine."

"What do you mean, sir?" the minister asked.

"All the books that have made Charles Oliver Farnsworth's name famous around the world, and which have enriched him beyond measure, are books written not by his hands, but by mine. We have known one another for years, Charles and I have, ever since boyhood. We are, in fact, cousins, and grew up together. It was that proximity of life and experience that made it easy for him to steal the product of my labors, the works I produced not for gain or commercial benefit, but for the sake of clinging to my own sanity."

"You're saying he's a plagiarist?" Billy said.

"Precisely. And I endured it for years, until at last I could stand no more of it, and vowed to find him and end his life."

"You see? He threatens me!" Farnsworth said, trembling. He tried to stand up, but almost fell, his legs so weak from his sickness. Billy went to him and helped him stand.

"Confess, you devil!" Church demanded. "I want the satisfaction of hearing the words come from your own lips! Admit that you have stolen my writings for years! Admit it!"

Laurel spoke. "It isn't true!" she said. "That isn't true, is it, Mr. Farnsworth?"

He turned his pale face to her. "I'm afraid it is true, my dear. My work . . . is not my work. It is true."

Laurel frowned and would not look at him.

Ulysses Church gripped his fists and raised them, side by side, looking toward the ceiling and laughing in loud triumph. "At last! At last the liar speaks the truth! I am vindicated! The truth is spoken!"

"Mister, you're bleeding," Billy said, having noticed a great patch of fresh blood appearing through Church's bandage. "You'd best settle yourself down before you do an injury to your own self."

Farnsworth, weak as he was, saw opportunity. He pushed himself away from the table and lunged at Church, who was distracted by his own celebration and did not see him coming. Farnsworth's weight pounded into Church, hitting him hard and making him fall backward. The back of his head struck the edge of a cabinet and he was knocked into a stupor. Farnsworth tried to rise but could make it no farther than his knees. Then he grew sick again, but there was nothing remaining in his stomach to heave up, and he hacked dryly.

Church's head was bleeding, but his patched bullet wound bled worse. He regained a bit of awareness and stared at his bleeding body, then lifted his head to look at Farnsworth.

"You have killed me," he said.

"Who shot you, you son of Satan?"

"A whore," said Church. "A whore who loved me."

"Die, Ulysses. Be gone. Die."

"I think . . . I shall," Church said, and slumped over to the side. He breathed a few moments more, then breathed no more.

"I think we should go," said the reverend. "And though it may sound odd for me to say this, I think we should keep all that has happened here to ourselves. I can see nothing gained in presenting it to the world."

Billy nodded. He wanted only to be through with all of this.

The outside door opened and Dr. Carlyle walked in, surprised to find his office occupied by so many. He looked worried until he saw his father.

"Your patient has hurt himself, I think," the reverend said, gesturing toward the deceased Ulysses Church.

"Dear God," the doctor murmured. "I warned him not to move about." Then he looked at Farnsworth, who had managed to pull himself up to his feet again, leaning on the examination table. "You are ill, sir?"

"I am."

"Who are you?"

"I am Charles Oliver Farnsworth."

"The writer?"

Farnsworth glanced at the others and seemed to be finding it hard to speak. "So is my reputation, at any rate."

The doctor nodded. "Then this, sir, I think is yours." He brought out from beneath his arm a familiar metal case, still bent partly open from the earlier storm, papers showing through the gap.

"Where . . . how . . ."

"It was in the possession of a man who I am afraid did not survive the storm," the doctor said. "A local bookseller."

Farnsworth claimed his manuscript and began to weep. He slumped back onto the table.

"Let me examine you, sir," said Dr. Carlyle. "You appear to be in need of care."

The others left the room and waited outside on the street of the storm-damaged town. At length Farnsworth, looking stronger already, appeared and the group headed back to the Rev. Carlyle's house.

They talked along the way of many things, anything but Farnsworth's writings and the ugly truths that had been revealed in his last encounter with his kinsman-enemy. They talked mostly of Laurel and the fact that surgery could correct her crippled state, if only she could obtain it.

That night, when Laurel went to bed as one of several guests lingering in the Rev. Carlyle's home, she slept in a deep peace and state of joy. The hope had been fulfilled, the sought-after promise made by Charles Farnsworth.

She and her father would travel to Chicago the next month. She would see Dr. Price in Chicago, and she would have her surgery.

And the bill for the miracle would go to Charles Oliver Farnsworth, to be paid for by proceeds from his newest book, soon to be completed.

CAMERON JUDD

BEGGAR'S GULCH

Life hasn't been easy for Matt McAllison. After avenging his father's brutal murder, he narrowly escapes a Kansas lynch mob. He flees to Colorado and finds work as a cowpuncher with the famous Jernigan outfit. Then things finally take a turn for the better. He even falls in love with the ranch owner's beautiful daughter, Melissa. But now, just as his life seems to be going well for a change, a mysterious band of outlaws has kidnapped Melissa. And one of the outlaws just might be Matt's best friend. There's only one thing left for Matt to do—strap on his guns and head back out on the vengeance trail!

Behold a Red Horse

Cotton Smith

After the Civil War, Ethan Kerry carved out the Bar K cattle spread with little more than hard work and fierce courage—and the help of his younger, slow-witted brother, Luther. But now the Bar K is in serious trouble. Ethan's loan was called in and the only way he can save the spread is if he can drive a herd from central Texas to Kansas. Ethan will need more than Luther's help this time—because Ethan has been struck blind by a kick from an untamed horse. His one slim hope has come from a most unlikely source—another brother, long thought dead, who follows the outlaw trail. Only if all three brothers band together can they save the Bar K . . . if they don't kill each other first.

___4894-9 $4.99 US/$5.99 CAN

THE SMOKY YEARS

Alan LeMay

The cattle barons. They were tough, weathered men like Dusty King and Lew Gordon, who had sweated and worked along the great cattle trails to form a partnership whose brand was burned on herds beyond measure. they had fought hard for what they had. . . and they would fight even harder to keep it. And they know a fight is coming. It is as thick in the wind as trail dust. Newcomers like Ben Thorpe are moving in, desperate to get their hands on the miles and miles of grazing land—land that King and Gordon want, and that Thorpe needs to survive. No one knows how the war will end, but one thing is certain—only one empire can survive.